MOTOR BOAT BOYS DOWN THE DANUBE

BY

LOUIS ARUNDEL

The Motorboat Boys Down The Danube

CHAPTER I

FOUR CHUMS ABROAD

"So this is the famous Budapest, is it, the twin cities of the blue Danube we've been hearing so much about?"

"Huh! doesn't strike me as so very much of a wonderful place. When you come to think of it, little old New York and Brooklyn can beat it all hollow so far as bustle and business go; even Chicago would run it a hot race."

"Now that's just like you, George Rollins, always ready to find fault, and throw cold water on everything. No wonder they've called you 'Doubting George' this long time back. There's always a flaw somewhere, you believe, and so you look for it right along."

"Between you and me, Buster, I don't think he ever will be cured of that nasty habit. Why can't he see the bright side of things once in a while, and be an optimist, like our chum and commodore, Jack Stormways?"

"Oh, you ought to know by this time, Josh, a leopard can't change its spots. I reckon our friend George here has spasms of reform once in just so often; but his weakness is ground in, and his resolves collapse, so he goes back to his old ways again."

"You don't say, Buster? Kindly take pity on my ignorance and tell me what there is so wonderful about this old Hungarian capital perched on the banks of the Danube and joined by bridges? I'm willing to have the scales taken from my eyes."

"Oh, well, first there's the river itself, not dirty water like most of our streams over in the States, but clear, and almost the color of the blue sky overhead."

"Sounds fine, Buster. Good for you; go ahead and open his blind eyes some more. It was always George's way to have his nose down over the engine of his Wireless motorboat, and never see a blessed thing around him. Hit him again for his mother, Buster."

"Then look at the clear atmosphere; the picturesque buildings hanging over the river banks; the queer shaped boats running back and forth; the remarkable costumes of these Magyars; and last, but far from least, that glorious August sunset painting the little clouds in the west crimson and green and gold. I tell you it's a scream of a place, if you've got any eyes in your head."

"Buster, you're a wonder at word painting, though I reckon you cribbed some of that stuff from the guide book. What do you say to it now, old If and But and Maybe?"

"Why, it looks good enough, I own up, fellows, but chances are all this is only on the surface. Scratch the veneer off when you go ashore to-morrow, and prowl around, and you'll find Budapest just as rotten at the core as Chicago."

"Don't waste any more words on the growler, Buster. There's such a thing as casting pearls before swine, you know—not saying that our chum here is really and truly a hog; but all the same he grunts like one. Let's talk about our own affairs."

"Wonder if Jack will fetch a sheaf of letters back from the postoffice? And say, I'm just a little mite anxious to learn how that spat between Serbia and Austria is going to turn out."

"All of us are, Buster, and have been ever since we read how the Grand Duke who was the latest heir to the Austrian throne after Francis Joseph was murdered with his wife by some Serbian hothead conspirators."

"Oh, as far as that goes, Josh, I figure that the game little bantam will have to take water and back down, after all this strutting around, just to show that Serbians have pluck."

"Don't be too sure of that, fellows," put in George; "you mustn't forget that Russia, yes, and France, too, are back of Serbia. There may be something more come out of this rattling of sabres in their scabbards than only a tempest in a teapot."

"Then it would be Russia and France against the two Teuton States," remarked the boy answering to the suggestive name of Buster; "and knowing how the Kaiser has been getting his country ready for a scrap this long while, I'd bet on them to turn the trick."

George, despite his failings, seemed to have read up on the matter and be pretty well posted on facts.

"But there's always a big chance it wouldn't stop there," he announced, with an air of importance; "other countries would sooner or later be drawn into the scramble, because everybody believes there's going to be an Armageddon or great world war before the era of peace finally comes along."

"Just what do you mean?" demanded Josh.

"There's Great Britain, for instance; she's bound to France in some way, and may have to shy her castor into the ring. Then her ally in the East, Japan, may choose to knock out Germany's holding in China, just to oblige. Besides, Italy must show her hand, and for one I can't believe she'll stand for her old enemy, Austria. And last, but not least, there's Turkey, hand in glove with Germany, besides all those scrappy little Balkan States, from Greece to Bulgaria and Rumania, who will fight just as they think their interests lie."

"Whee! but it would be a grand smash-up if all that comes off!" ejaculated Buster. "I'd sure hate to pay the bills. It'd take me some time to get enough of the long green together I sure reckon."

"Seems to me it's high time for Jack to be showing up," ventured Josh. "I hope he hasn't run up against any trouble, being unable to speak even ten words of German, while the Magyar tongue is a sealed book to him."

"I hinted to Jack that perhaps I'd better be the one to go," said George, modestly, "because I know German fairly well; but he only laughed, and said there were lots of ways of communicating with a Hungarian as long as both parties had their hands to use and could wink and nod."

"Oh, well, while we're waiting for him here on our old powerboat that we chartered," said Buster, with a resigned air, "I'm going to take time to make out a list of groceries we want to lay in while we're at the capital. Goodness knows if we'll have a half-way decent chance to buy anything worth eating again before we strike the Serbian border, and then push on through Rumania to the Black Sea."

George and Josh also sought comfortable seats where they could lounge and watch in a lazy fashion the bustling scene around them; for there were dozens of quaint sights to be seen if one only used his eyes.

While the three lads are thus employed, awaiting the coming of their comrade who had gone to get their mail at the general postoffice, a few words of explanation concerning them may not come amiss.

These four boys belonged to a motorboat club over in the Middle West, their home being on the upper Mississippi River. There were two other members, who had not made the trip abroad, by name Herb Dickson and Jimmy Brannagan, the latter a ward of Jack Stormways' father.

Buster, of course, had another name, which was Nicholas Longfellow. Nature had in a way played a sad joke on the boy, for, while a Longfellow by family relation, he was also pudgy and fat, always wheezing when exerting himself, but as jolly as could be, full of good nature, and willing to go to any trouble to help a friend, yes, or even an enemy.

Josh Purdue had a strain of the Yankee in him, for he was as sharp as a steel trap, though perfectly honest. As an all-round comrade Josh could not very well be excelled.

George Rollins was a good-enough chap too, though he complained at times, and was so inclined to want to be shown that his friends had dubbed him "Old Missouri" and "Doubting George."

These six boys had gone through a good many lively times together, as they possessed three motorboats of different models, called the Wireless, a cracky craft built for racing, and which gave George, the skipper, much trouble; the Tramp, which Jack commanded; and the beamy Comfort, run by Herb Dickson.

It would be utterly impossible for us to undertake to mention a tithe of their interesting and thrilling escapades while cruising in these boats. If the reader who has made their acquaintance for the first time in this volume desires to know more about these happenings, he is referred to the six earlier books in the Motorboat Boys' Series, all of which can be easily procured.

As to just how the interesting quartette of wide-awake American boys came to be running down the historical Danube River in the late summer of nineteen-fourteen, that can be easily explained.

Some of their parents were well-to-do, and as school would not begin this year until some time in October or November, it was at first suggested in a spirit of fun, and then debated as an actual possibility, that they coax their folks to let them go abroad for a season.

Needless to say that as the lads had considerable money in the treasury, thanks to their having been instrumental in capturing some bold bank robbers who had run away with the funds of an institution, they were finally able to gain their folks' consent.

Then came the question of what they would like to do most of all. By this time they had come to be such cruisers that they could not bear the thought of following in the footsteps of the general run of European tourists. Any one could read all about the cities in the magazine accounts, as well as the many books of foreign travel.

It was Jack who made a startling proposition that caught the fancy of the other three from the first.

He had lately been reading an account of a canoe trip made by an English gentleman all the way down the Danube from its source in Germany not far from the Rhine, through Austria-Hungary, along the Serbian border, and then through Rumania until he finally reached the Black Sea, and brought up at Constantinople.

The account was so vividly written up that it appealed strongly to Jack, and his proposition was that they make their way to some place further down the beautiful river than his starting point, charter some kind of a motorboat, and continue the voyage. They could thus get to the Turkish capital in good time after a most interesting trip, take a steamer to London, and come home in that way.

Well, the more they talked it over the stronger grew the inclination to enjoy a water voyage through a most interesting country, the praises of which they had seen sung in many an account they managed to unearth at the library.

Eventually this was just what the daring quartette had done. They were lucky enough to get hold of a pretty fair powerboat that would accommodate four sleepers with some crowding. This they had fitted up to suit themselves, for long experience in camping out had made them wise in many particulars. And, Buster considered this the most important part of the whole business, they had found a little kerosene blue-flame stove something like those they owned at home, upon which many of their future meals were likely to be cooked.

The party had only been a short time on the way when they brought up at the Hungarian capital, where it was planned to spend a couple of days prying around; for they had reason to believe they would run across no large city save Belgrade in Serbia until they crossed the Black Sea and came to Constantinople.

As often happens, the best laid plans often go astray, and, looking back to former scenes, the four chums could pick out several other instances when this had happened to them.

Buster had just finished his long list of eatables, in which he jotted down everything that appealed to his voracious appetite, when Josh was heard saying he had glimpsed Jack coming. All of them therefore jumped up to greet the bearer of the mailbag, being greatly interested in news from the home folks.

"Something has happened, as sure as you live!" exclaimed Josh as the fourth member of the little party drew closer; "look at Jack's face, will you? He couldn't be more solemn if he had been told he was going to be hung to-morrow."

"No bad news from across the sea, I hope, Jack?" faltered Buster.

Jack Stormways, who was a resolute looking young fellow, a born leader among boys, shook his head and allowed a faint smile to steal across his sober countenance.

"I'm glad to say it isn't that, fellows," he told them; "but all Budapest is in a frightful uproar just now, and it's a question if our lovely voyage doesn't come to a sudden end right here."

"Great Cæsar's ghost! What's happened now, Jack?" cried Josh, looking alarmed.

"Only this, and you can guess what it means in Europe," Jack announced. "Germany declared war on Russia last night, and her army is said to be already marching into neutral Belgium to strike France in the back, and take Paris!"

CHAPTER II

THE NEWS OF WAR AT BUDAPEST

When Jack made this astounding statement the other three stared at him as though they could hardly believe he was not joking. But then Jack seldom attempted to play a practical prank; besides, they could see that he was seriously disposed, and evidently grappling with one of the largest propositions that had ever faced him.

"Then it means a world war has begun, does it?" gasped Buster presently, when he could catch his breath again.

"That's what it's bound to result in," Jack told him. "The cry of 'wolf' has been heard for the last time, and now the beast has come!"

"But will Great Britain and all the other nations jump in?" demanded George.

"Not jump in, but find themselves dragged in, in spite of their horror of war. This thing has been hanging fire a long while, but every little while there would be signs of what lay under the surface. Lots of people predicted it was bound to come sooner or later, and that the destinies of every world power would have to be settled once and for all by the sword."

"Then all other wars will be baby play beside this one," Josh declared, "with the wonderful modern arms they've got. Millions of men must be killed before the end comes, and old Europe will never know herself, such great changes in border lines are bound to take place."

"But what of us?" asked George.

"That's what we've got to decide right away," Jack announced. "We live thousands of miles away from the scene of hostilities, and our neutral country may not be pulled into the whirlpool; but here we are in Austria-Hungary that is now in a state of war with Serbia, Montenegro, Russia and France, with other countries to hear from. What ought we do about it?"

"Let's tell the Kaiser we won't stand for any of this funny business," Buster went on to say, pretending to look very important, though there was a quizzical gleam in his eyes at the same time; "let him know he's got to sheathe that sword of his in double-quick time, or America will get mad."

"Much the Kaiser would care for a dozen Americas," jeered George. "Germany armed can defy the whole world, and as for our great big country, we're only a second China, don't you know—plenty of people, much talk, but able to do next door to nothing."

"I say it would be a beastly shame if we had to quit now before hardly getting started," asserted Josh, indignantly.

"Go on, the rest of you, for I want to hear everybody's opinion," urged Jack.

"But if the whole of Austria is on a war footing, what chance would we have to continue our lovely voyage?" George wanted to know. "As like as not we'd be arrested, because they'd call us spies trying to find a way to invade the country through the back door."

"One for keeping on, and another against it, which is a stand-off," remarked Jack; "how about you, Buster?"

"Gee whilikens! I hardly know where I'm at," muttered the fat chum, rubbing the tip of his nose in bewilderment; "fact is I'm about ready to do whatever the rest of you say."

"In other words, you're on the fence, I take it," sneered George; "if there's anything I dislike it's to run across a jellyfish, something that has no opinions of its own. There, that's one for you fellows calling me swine. But how about you, Jack? We ought to know what you think about it all."

"That's right," agreed Josh eagerly, for he could see that their future movements were likely to be controlled by whatever Jack said, since with a tie his vote would be the deciding factor.

"I'll be frank with you fellows," Jack continued soberly. "We've gone to a whole lot of trouble and expense to get started on this cruise, and I hate like everything to give it up."

"Hear! hear!" came from Josh, with a tinge of growing triumph in his voice.

"When I think of all that we'd have to go through with to get back to London the way we came I feel like saying we ought to try and keep right on down the river. The greatest danger to us would come from approaching the fighting region around Northern France and Belgium."

Even George seemed to be hanging on Jack's words as though, after all, his ideas of prudence might be undergoing a change.

"We could go ashore right away," Jack continued, "and buy what stuff we need, for I see Bumpus is holding a list in his hand, and we know him well enough to feel sure he's omitted nothing worth while having."

"That settles it, then," burst out Josh. "You hear, George, you're outvoted three to one. We go on our way, snapping our fingers under the nose of every Magyar who feels like questioning our right to cruise down the beautiful blue Danube."

"Oh, well, move we make it unanimous then," snapped George, which proved that, after all, his objections could only have been skin-deep, and were offered more in a spirit of contrariness than seriously.

"Here are letters for every one," remarked Jack; "but if you take my advice you'll keep them until after we've had supper. There's a whole lot to be done before night settles down."

"Jack, you've been ashore, and mebbe now you happened to notice a good grocery store where we could pick up what we need in the line of grub," and as he asked this Buster waved his formidable list before him.

"It happens that I did just that same thing, and, better still, the place is only a short distance away from here. From the glance I took at it I reckon we could get about everything we want, provided we're willing to take them in the Hungarian style of putting up the packages."

"Oh," decided Buster, "so far as that goes, a rose by any other name would smell just as sweet. I'd be willing to forget the trade names of the oatmeal, hominy, and such things I'm used to seeing, if the contents of the packages turned out to be as good."

"All right, Buster," continued the other, "suppose we start out right away and do our shopping. I suppose if we buy for cash they'll send the things around here to this boat builder's wharf where we had permission to tie up during our stay here."

Everybody looked pleased. It was as if a dreadful load had been suddenly lifted from their hearts. They would never have been fully satisfied to abandon their trip down the Danube on such short notice. In times to come they would very likely call themselves silly to be frightened off so easily by what might turn out to be only a shadow of coming trouble.

Buster proved himself willing enough by scrambling ashore. In fact, when the question of eating was concerned no one could ever accuse the fat boy of shirking his duty; as Josh said, "When the dinner horn blew Buster was always Johnny-on-the-spot," though truth to tell the said Josh often ran a race with his comrade at table.

"I don't suppose you'll be needing a German scholar along with you to do the bargaining?" suggested George pompously.

Buster chuckled at hearing that.

"Don't you worry about us, George," he advised the other, "we can get through all right. As long as I've got eyes and can smell things I reckon I'll be able to pick out what we want most. And money talks, George, better than some people's German."

"Oh, well, they say a prophet never is appreciated in his own country," sighed George; "but all the same I'm going to practice up in my German, because it may serve us well sooner or later. If you fellows get pinched, send us word and I'll hurry around to the police station to explain matters."

"How kind you are, George; but I'm afraid after they heard your fine German they'd put you behind the bars for murdering the language."

With that parting shot Buster hurried away, leaving Josh shaking his sides with laughter, for they did love to get a crack at George, who was always complaining and throwing cold water on every plan.

Jack led the way, for, having been already over the ground, he could serve in the capacity of pilot.

"Listen, Buster," he said impressively as they walked along toward the nearby street, "from now on we want to let everybody know that we're American boys, and not English, you understand."

"What's the idea, Jack? Up to now a lot of people have taken us for English, and we've let it go at that without taking the bother to explain, because there's always been a warm friendly feeling between the Austrians and the English."

"That's right, Buster, but if Great Britain gets into this big scrap you can see that she'll be up against the soldiers of Austria-Hungary as well as those of the Kaiser. So from now on stand up for your colors. We're Americans every time, and don't you forget it."

Buster evidently saw the point, for he promised to faithfully observe the counsel of his mate, in whom he placed the utmost reliance.

They soon reached the store which Jack had noticed. It was quite an extensive establishment, and there could be little doubt but that everything needful on Buster's list might be procured there. If some of the items chanced to be lacking, their place could be filled with others equally attractive, Jack felt sure.

By great good luck the proprietor could speak and read English. This made it very easy for the purchasers. He also promised to have the goods delivered inside of an hour, and said he knew the boatyard well.

When Jack went to pay for their purchases he had only English money. He thought the merchant looked at him a little more closely, and considered that this was a very good opportunity to prove their nationality. So he took out a letter he had just received, which bore the home postmark across in America. This he showed, as well as one Buster also produced, as proof of his assertion that they were Americans, and not English.

"Nothing like getting your hand in," he told Buster later on when they were making their way back to where the boat was tied up.

"And come to think of it," added the other with sudden vehemence, "I believe I've got a little silk edition of Old Glory stowed away somewhere in my bundle. I just chucked the same in, thinking we might want to fasten it to our boat; but up to this minute it's slipped my mind. How'd it do to make use of it, Jack?"

"Splendid idea," commented the other.

"As long as that waves in the breeze nobody can mistake our nationality; even if George keeps on trying to talk that silly German of his. He makes such a mess of it that some of these people may think we're spies out to learn all about the fortifications of the lower Danube."

Upon their arrival at the boat the others questioned them concerning the success of their undertaking. Josh also wanted to know if they had managed to pick up any further news concerning the great struggle that had begun.

"We went after grub," Buster told him severely, "and that being the case, you needn't expect that we would waste our precious time jabbering about a silly old war, would you? If you do you've got another guess coming. And say, we got everything on my list, would you believe it, or something that was just as good."

"Huh! I can see why you're grinning so happily, Buster," sneered George; "you're contemplating many a fine feed ahead."

"We're all in the same boat, George," sang out Buster blithely; "and when the tocsin calls us to supper I notice that as a rule you're never hanging far in the rear. Considering the difference in our heft, I take it I've got a bird's appetite compared with you and Josh here—pound for pound."

"Well, it's getting twilight, so suppose we start in with that same supper," Jack ventured to say. "For one I'm willing to admit that an afternoon humming down the river has given me a ferocious appetite; and I'm not ashamed to declare it, either."

Buster needed no second invitation. Time had been when the fat boy hardly knew how to cook a rasher of bacon properly; but his love of eating had inspired him to pick up fresh knowledge, with the result that he now stood in a class by himself.

Perhaps Josh and George, wishing to shirk much of their share of the culinary operations, flattered Buster more than was really necessary. They imposed upon his good nature in this way outrageously; but since the stout youth seemed to really enjoy handling the saucepans and skillet, Jack interposed no objections.

Supper was soon ready, though they had to light the lanterns before they could sit down at the little adjustable table, which, when not in use, could be slung up against the wall of the cabin and the space it occupied utilized as sleeping quarters for one of the crew.

After that they sat around talking in low tones and covering a wide range of subjects as usual in their conversation, from the folks at home, numerous former escapades that came to mind, to the terrible conflict that apparently promised to engulf the whole of Europe in its thrall.

Then a vehicle came into the boatyard and the stores were taken aboard. When they had been stowed away in temporary places Jack declared that he meant to open his letter from home and enjoy the contents.

Of course, this reminded the others that they too had news from those dear ones now so far away, and for a long time the four sat there, lost in contemplation of distant scenes brought close to them by those envelopes and their contents.

Later on they lay down to secure what sleep was possible. As a rule, after the first night afloat all of them had little difficulty about sleeping; but it seemed that on this occasion they turned and tossed considerably more than usual before settling down. Perchance it was the thrilling news they had heard that afternoon that made them so restless; or it may have been a premonition of coming difficulties that kept them awake; but morning came and found them far from refreshed.

CHAPTER III

TAKING CHANCES

"Better take a little turn ashore, Josh and George, while I'm getting breakfast ready," advised Buster; "you'd hate to say you'd passed through Budapest without even setting foot in the city."

"If you go, be careful not to get lost," added Jack, looking as though almost tempted to veto the arrangement; but George proudly declared he felt sure of being able to find his way about.

"Don't be more than half an hour at the most, fellows," sang out Buster after the couple, and they waved their hands at him as if they understood.

About the time breakfast was ready Jack went ashore to look for the absent ones, but there was as yet no sign of them. In fact, the two who were left aboard had more than half finished their meal and were becoming really worried when the others made their appearance.

George looked a trifle chagrined, while Josh was chuckling to himself.

"What's the joke? Tell us, Josh," demanded Buster.

"Oh, yes, hurry up and give him the full particulars," sneered George, looking daggers at his companion.

"Why, you see, George here tried some of his German on a gendarme we happened to meet," explained Josh between gurgles. "Say, you ought to have seen how surprised that cop looked. I'm afraid George got his nouns twisted and called him some sort of bad name. Anyhow, he was for taking us to the lock-up; but I managed to soothe him down some by showing him my letters with the American postmarks on them, and letting a silver coin slip into his hand. But he shook his head and looked as if he could eat poor George. All the way back George has been racking his brain trying to understand what it was he really called that uniformed gendarme. I rather think it stood for pig."

"Well, let that rest, will you, Josh?" growled George. "What I'm most interested in just now is pig of another kind, for I see Buster has fried some bacon for us. Mistakes will happen in the best regulated families, they say, and I own up I'm afraid I did get my nouns slightly mixed."

"Slightly!" echoed Josh, with a shrug of his shoulders. "Well, if the boys could only have seen how that big cop scowled at you they'd have had a fit."

As Josh was also hungry, he wasted no more time in explanations, and so the incident was forgotten for the present. Later on it would doubtless give

Josh occasion for considerable additional merriment and be the cause for more or less acrimonious conversation between the pair.

While they were eating Jack proceeded to settle with the owner of the boatyard for the accommodations, for a bargain had been struck with him. People over in old Europe are not apt to do things without a consideration, especially when tourists are concerned.

By the time George and Josh had finished their morning meal everything was in order for making a start.

"It's pretty tough to be running away like this without having a chance to see what sort of movies they have over here in Budapest," complained George, who was known to be a steady attendant at the little theatre in his home town, where all manner of dramas, as well as world-wide views, were nightly screened.

"So far as that goes," Josh told him, "they're pretty much all alike here and at home. Chances are you'd see some cowboy pictures of the wild and woolly West; for they do say those are the ones they like best abroad. They know all about Buffalo Bill over here. You know we saw an Austrian edition of some highly colored story about his imaginary exploits hanging up when we passed that book stall."

Working the boat free from all entanglements, they were soon afloat once more on the river. The motor had started working as though it meant to do good service. Jack himself as a rule took charge of the machinery, not but that George knew all about such things, but he had a decided failing, which was to "monkey" with things even when they were running satisfactorily, and thus bring about sudden stoppages through his experiments.

"Look at the beautiful bridge we're going to pass under," sang out Buster presently. "It makes me think of one we saw in London."

"There's a bunch of Austrian officers walking across," said Josh, "and see how one of them is pointing to us now."

"Bet you they're suspicious of us right away, and mean to order us to go back," said George disconsolately.

"Rats!" scoffed Buster. "Don't you see they're only admiring our little flag?— that's all. I've got the same fastened in the stern, where it can show well. I only wish it was five times as big, that's all. But it stands for what we are— true-blooded Americans, every one of us."

The officers even leaned over the parapet of the bridge to stare at the boat as it passed under. When the boys looked back a minute or so later they saw that the uniformed Hungarians had hurriedly crossed over and were now gazing after them.

"Shows how seldom Old Glory is ever seen in these parts," said Josh, "for they hardly know what to make of it. If I had my way, can you guess what I'd do? Make the flag of the free so well known and respected that everywhere people'd kowtow to the same and take off their hats."

"Now they're hurrying off the bridge, seems like, as if they'd just remembered an engagement somewhere," reported Buster.

"I only hope they don't start any sort of trouble for us, that's all," George went on to say, but, finding that no one seemed to be paying any sort of attention to his grumbling, he stopped short, as his kind always do.

Jack held the wheel and guided the boat along through the numerous mazes of moving river craft. He was a skillful pilot and could be depended on to mind his business every time. Unlike George, Jack was plain and practical, whereas the other never seemed satisfied with what he had, but was always trying to better conditions, often to his own and others' discomfort, as well as possible delay.

By degrees they were now leaving the twin cities behind them, and the river began to appear more open and free to travel. The boys, as usual, were calling each other's attention to such features of the landscape that attracted their admiration, or it might be some of the buildings they passed.

All of them were on the watch for special sights, and in this way the time passed rapidly. The little motor was a very good one, and chugged away faithfully as it had continued to do hour after hour ever since the start, which was made far down the river below Vienna.

They overtook other vessels frequently, since the Danube is navigable for the greater part of its long course. Rising away over in Germany near the border of Luxemburg, it winds its sinuous way through the greater part of Germany and Austria-Hungary, strikes the Serbian border, turns sharply to the east, and then touches Bulgarian territory, forms the dividing line between Rumania and Bulgaria, then crosses the former monarchy, and serves as a border between Rumania and Russia, to finally empty into the Black Sea.

It is by long odds the greatest river in Europe, and in all the world there can be found no stream upon whose borders live so many different nationalities. That was one reason Jack Stormways had yearned to cruise down the Danube; and he was even now trying to get all the pleasure possible out of the trip, though the clouds had arisen so early in the venture.

Budapest was now far in the rear, though they could see the smoke that arose in a few localities, coming from certain factories producing articles for which the Hungarian capital is famous.

Josh happened to notice about this time that George seemed to be amusing himself by shading his eyes with one hand and looking backward.

"What now, old croaker?" he ventured to say. "Do you imagine you see a patrol boat chasing after us hotfooted, with orders to bring us back and throw us in a black dungeon, charged with being desperate spies?"

"Laugh as much as you want to," retorted George stubbornly, "but all the same there is a boat hustling along after us."

"You don't say!" gibed Josh, without bothering to turn his head to look. "Well, since when have we taken out a mortgage on the Danube, please tell me? I guess it's free cruising ground for anybody who can afford to own a steam yacht, or even a common little dinky motorboat."

"She certainly is coming hand over fist after us," asserted Buster.

"Well, the river is sure wide enough for two, and when she comes up we'll give her a chance to pass us by. Whew! but I'm sleepy, if you want to know it," and Josh yawned and stretched, but still declined to bother turning his head.

A little while later George again made a remark.

"Now that they're coming closer, I believe I can see several people in uniforms aboard that swift little boat."

Jack took a look on hearing this.

"You're right there, George," he assented; "but then there's nothing to hinder Magyar officers going on the river when they choose. In fact, I imagine they pass plenty of their time that way when off duty."

Josh could not hold out after that any longer, but condescended to lazily turn and indifferently survey the approaching craft.

"Oh, she's a dandy for speed, all right," he frankly admitted, "and could make circles around our old tub if the skipper wanted. Yes, those are soldiers on board, I'll admit, but how can you decide that they want to overhaul us, I'd like to know?"

"I'm only guessing when I say that," acknowledged George; "but now that I look sharper it strikes me one of those officers is the tall chap wearing the feather in his hat that we noticed on the bridge. How about it, Jack?"

"He looks like that man, but then there are probably scores in Budapest who wear that same kind of hat, Alpine style. He's probably an officer of the mountaineer corps, those fellows from the Carnic Alps who can do such wonderful stunts in scaling dizzy heights."

"Well, we must soon know if there's going to be any sort of a row," said George, "because in ten minutes or less they'll overtake us."

"There must be no row, remember, boys," advised Jack. "If we attempted to resist arrest we'd soon be trapped, for they would send word down-river way about us by telegraph or telephone, and officers would be on the watch for us all along the route. Don't forget that."

"Paste it in your hat, George," advised Josh, "for I reckon you're the only one in the bunch liable to make trouble. If they want to take me back and give me free lodging, I'll go as meek as Mary's little lamb. But whatever you do, George, please be careful how you fling that German of yours around loose. If you called one of those fiery Hungarian officers a donkey by mistake I think he'd want to run you through the ribs with his sword."

"Huh! wait and see. That German you pretend to make so much fun about may some day keep you from being hung or stood up against a blank wall. Stranger things than that have happened, let me tell you, Josh Purdue."

"They keep pushing us right along," announced Buster, beginning to feel quite an interest in the affair by this time.

"Get ready to give them the right of way, Jack," jeered Josh. "We wouldn't want to act greedy, you know, and claim the whole river. And when they whiz past look out you don't get splashed, Buster."

"Goodness! I hope you don't mean to say they might swamp us away out here in the middle of the river. But there, I know you're only being true to your name, Josh. Who's afraid? You don't get me to worrying any if I know it."

"Look again and see what's happening!" suddenly snapped George, with a ring of triumph in his voice.

"They're waving to us, for a fact!" admitted Buster. "Now what d'ye suppose that can be for, Jack?"

"Just saluting our little flag, mebbe," suggested the unconverted Josh.

"They are demanding that we pull up and wait for them, that's what!" asserted George, with a superior air that he liked to assume on occasions like this.

"Is he right there, Jack?" asked Buster eagerly.

"I think that's what is meant," assented the pilot and engineer of the powerboat the boys had chartered. "They are suspicious of us, and mean to have a look in before allowing us to proceed."

"But why should anybody be suspicious of four honest-looking boys out for a little fun?" demanded Josh. "We've met heaps of other people before now, and they acted just as nice as you please. I don't understand it."

"Well, you must remember," admonished Jack, "that something terrible has happened since yesterday morning. Every military man in Germany and Austria has been on needles and pins about this war business ever since Serbia defied Francis Joseph and some of her adventurers murdered the heir apparent to the Austrian throne. And now that war has broken out, they are all eager to show their fidelity to their country."

"But will you stop for them, Jack?" asked Josh.

"It would be foolish not to," he was told, "because you can see it's only a matter of ten minutes at most when they will have overhauled us. It pays to be courteous, especially, I'm told, when dealing with the military authorities over here. Besides, in war times they rule the roost."

"I guess they do all the time," muttered Josh; "but then you're right about it, Jack. We must get ready to show them just who and what we are. If they're sensible men they'll let us go on down the river as we've planned."

"And supposing they happen to be unreasonable men?" queried Buster.

"Oh, some of the dungeons may be large enough to hold you, perhaps," laughed George; "but I can see your finish on a diet of bread and water, mostly water. You will waste away to a shadow before you get out, Buster."

The other only gave him a scornful look, as much as to say he was not worrying any about that part of the game, for he knew he could rely on Jack to pull them all through safely.

So Jack shut off the power, and the clumsy but comfortable boat lay wallowing on the surface of the river, awaiting the coming of the speedy craft containing the Hungarian army officers.

CHAPTER IV

UNDER SUSPICION

Although every one tried to put the best face on the matter, afterwards more than one of the boys frankly confessed that his heart was beating furiously during that time when waiting for the speed boat to come up.

They were in a strange land, it must be remembered, and the habits of the Magyars were unfamiliar to them. More than this, war had just been declared, which was sure to mean that Austria-Hungary would be at handgrips with not only Serbia on the south, but great Russia as well.

They gathered at the stern of the boat and awaited whatever fate had in store for them. Josh was so much afraid even then that George might be tempted to try his American German on the Hungarian officers that he immediately made a suggestion.

"Remember, now, everybody keep still but Jack. That's meant for you, Buster, as well as George here. The rest of us are apt to get excited and do our case more harm than good if we butt in."

"I'm as mum as an oyster, Josh," said Buster readily.

"How about you, George?" demanded the other sternly.

"Oh, I'll promise all right," mumbled George, shaking his head; "but all the same, I do it under protest. You don't know what you may be missing when you put the muzzle on a fellow that way. But I'm used to being sat on, and I guess I can stand for it again."

Jack himself was pleased to hear Josh settle this. He had feared that George, who could make himself more or less of a busybody when he chose, might break in when the negotiations were well under way and possibly spoil the whole business.

But they would at least soon know the worst, for the other boat was coming on at great speed and about to draw alongside.

The man at the wheel knew his part of the business perfectly, for when the craft came together the bump was hardly noticeable.

There were just three of the Hungarian officers, all of them dressed in their attractive uniforms, with little capes hanging from their shoulders and their lower limbs encased in shiny boots with tassels. Indeed, Buster just stared at them in sheer admiration, for he thought he had never in all his life looked upon such handsome soldiers.

Apparently the tall one must have been the superior of the trio, for he took it upon himself to do the talking.

All of them were looking curiously at the four lads. They evidently hardly knew what to make of them, for, while outwardly Jack and his chums had the appearance of harmless young chaps off for a holiday, nevertheless in such dark times as now hung over the Fatherland it was not well to be too easily deceived. Spies must be abroad, under many disguises; and if so, why not playing the part of innocent tourists, was no doubt the question uppermost in each of their minds.

Then the tall officer said something. His voice was filled with authority and his face frowning, but of course none of the boys could understand a word he uttered, for the Magyar tongue was a sealed book to them.

They could, of course, give a pretty good guess that he was asking who they were and what they might be doing there. George sighed as though it nearly broke his ardent heart to be deprived of this golden opportunity to air some of his German. He had perhaps managed to remember certain words that would serve to partly explain the situation; but a savage nudge from Josh caused him to shut his teeth fiercely together and get a fresh grip on himself.

Then Jack tried an experiment.

"We do not understand what you say, because none of us can speak the language. We only know English. We would be glad to explain everything if you could understand what we tell you."

The tall man listened attentively and then immediately turned to his comrades to say something to them. It was just as if he remarked, "Didn't I tell you they must be English?" for Jack caught the concluding word.

Then, turning again to them, the officer went on:

"Certainly we can speak English as well as is necessary. We have many tourists in our country each summer. I myself have a number of very good friends among the English, though when we meet again it may be as bitter enemies."

Jack saw that there need be no further trouble in explaining matters. He felt decidedly relieved over the sudden change in the situation. Only George frowned, for possibly he had been entertaining a forlorn hope that in the end Jack might have to call on him to save the day, and now he knew that chance was doomed.

"I am glad you can understand what I want to tell you," Jack proceeded. "In the first place, we are not English at all, but from America."

Again the three Hungarians exchanged significant looks. Evidently they did not know whether to believe the assertion or not.

"We have great regard for America," the tall man went on to say, "for many of our countrymen are there, making an honest living and helping to support their kin on this side of the water. Of course, then, you can show us your passports?"

"Certainly, sir, and with pleasure," responded Jack.

His words served as the signal to the others. Every fellow immediately hastened to dive into his breast pocket and produce the necessary paper, which was always kept in an especially safe place for fear of trouble in case of its being lost.

The officer took the sheaf of papers and proceeded to critically examine the passports, as though looking for signs of fraud. Buster watched him anxiously. He had heard that when war came upon a country all ordinary protection for tourists is annulled, and even passports may not be worth the paper they are written on.

Greatly to Buster's relief he saw that the tall officer did not look at them so ferociously after he had scanned the papers, which he now handed back to Jack in a bunch.

"They seem to be perfectly correct, so far as I can see," he proceeded to say; "but perhaps you would not mind explaining what your object is in coming down the Danube in this powerboat?"

"I'll be only too glad to do that, sir," Jack announced, with one of his winning smiles that always caused people to feel kindly toward him. "Over in our own country we have three motorboats, with which six of us in times past have made many exciting cruises along the great rivers, and the coast as well."

The officer nodded his head, while his face lighted up. Evidently he could appreciate the love for adventure that induced these healthy specimens of boyhood to want to be in the open air all they could. Perhaps whenever he had the chance for an outing he might have been found off in the mountains, hunting the wild boar, or it might be in pursuit of the nimble chamois.

"When we had a chance to come to Europe this summer," continued Jack, "we decided that the thing we would like best of all would be a long trip down the beautiful blue Danube. I had just been reading an account of a cruise taken by an Englishman from near the source down to the Black Sea. While we couldn't spare the time for all that, we could come to Vienna, find where a suitable boat could be chartered half-way to Budapest, and make our start there. And, sir, that is what we have done. We are now just two days on the way."

"I admire your courage, as well as your choice of the Danube for your trip. Many a voyage have I taken on its waters when I was younger. But how long have you been at Budapest, may I ask?"

Jack knew that there was only one way to treat such a questioner, and that was by being perfectly frank with him.

"We only arrived late yesterday afternoon, to tell the truth, sir," he admitted.

"But how comes it you are leaving so early the next morning?" asked the officer, with a little fresh suspicion in his manner. "We have a most beautiful and renowned city here, and travelers usually find it difficult to tear themselves away from it, even after a stay of days. You seem to have been in a great hurry."

"We own up that we are, sir," continued Jack. "You see, the first thing I did on arriving was to hasten to the postoffice for our letters from home. It was then that I realized the city was in a feverish state of excitement. I suspected what must have happened, for we heard rumors when above. I managed to learn that war had been declared by Germany on Russia, which would mean for Austria-Hungary, too. And after we had talked it all over we decided that it would be best for us not to waste any time here, but hurry along our way."

"Would you mind showing me those letters?" asked the officer.

"With the greatest of pleasure, sir," Jack told him. "Boys, hand him the last ones you received, please."

The other took them as they were thrust out. He examined the postmarks as if making sure of the dates, and also read each name in turn. Then he deliberately opened that belonging to Jack and seemed to be glancing over it, though the boy felt rather surprised to see him do this.

Still, it was good to find the officer nodding his head as he gleaned something of the contents. At least he could see it was genuine, and that counted for a good deal.

"I am quite satisfied now that you are just what you claim to be—tourists, who have no connection with our enemies, or those who in a short time we must look on as such. You are wondering, no doubt, why I went so far as to pry into the contents of your letter from home, and I believe an explanation is due. To tell the truth, we rested under the belief that you were four desperate young Serbian youths, who were said to be on their way up the Danube bound for Vienna, with the mad intention of trying to assassinate our good kaiser, Francis Joseph, just as the Austrian heir apparent to the throne was killed not long ago."

Buster could not keep from giving a little gasp at hearing this. Really never before, so far as he knew, had he been taken for a desperado. He did not know whether to be ashamed or flattered. It would be something with which to thrill those boy comrades at home, if ever they were lucky enough to get safely back again.

"That would be a serious charge against us, I am sure," said Jack; "but it pleases us to know that you are now convinced we are not what you thought. Seeing four strangers in a boat, and all young at that, of course made you suspicious."

"The fact that you were headed down-stream puzzled us considerably," continued the officer, apparently willing to explain things in order to prove that he and his comrades were only doing their duty; "but we figured that something may have caused a change in plans, perhaps the breaking out of war, and that the four desperate Serbians were on the way back to their native land."

"After all, we should not be sorry for what has happened," diplomatic Jack went on to say, "since it has given us the pleasure of meeting three such excellent gentlemen. I hope, though, there need be no necessity for causing us to alter our plans, since our hearts are set on finishing the voyage, and we will never have the opportunity for visiting your great country again."

Every one of them held his breath while waiting for the officer to make a reply to this question. He looked around at the half circle of anxious faces and smiled indulgently. No doubt just then he put himself in their place and tried to realize how much it might mean to be simply let alone.

"I do not mean to demand that you turn back," he finally told Jack, "for that would really be exceeding my authority; but I would feel that I had not done my full duty if I did not warn you of the perils you will likely encounter below here. By the time you reach the Serbian border it is more than likely there will be desperate fighting going on between Hungarians and Serbians, for they are ready to-day to fly at one another's throat. You will find yourselves in great danger before you can pass the Iron Gate and enter Rumania."

Jack only smiled reassuringly at him.

"Thank you many times, sir, for taking enough interest in us to give that kind warning," he remarked warmly; "but we have passed through some pretty lively adventures in the past and always managed to come out safely.

We will try and be careful how we act when the time comes; and once past the Serbian border along the Danube we need fear little else."

"Well, I admire your boldness, while at the same time I fear you may be making a mistake. We will wish you a pleasant trip, and that you reach your goal in safety. What are your plans after arriving at the sea, may I ask?"

"We have arranged to send the boat back to the owner at our expense," explained Jack. "Then we will find some way of getting to Constantinople, where we hope to remain a short time, looking around. From there we go to Italy, and then back to London to sail for home about October fifteenth."

"Ah! what wonderful things may happen in those ten weeks!" remarked the officer, as though he might be trying to lift the veil that hid the future. "History will be in the making, I fear, and all Europe be torn up with the war clouds. But better so than the armed peace that has existed so long. A storm is necessary once in so often to clear the atmosphere which has become murky."

He thrust out his hand to Jack, who gladly seized it.

"May the best of luck follow you all the way, is the wish of myself and my comrades here," the tall officer told them as in turn he pressed each boy's hand, in which genial undertaking he was followed by the other pair, who, although taking no part in all the talking, had been earnest listeners.

Then the speed boat backed away, made a sweeping turn, and was soon heading up the Danube again. The boys waved their hats to the three gaily dressed Hungarian soldiers seated in the other craft, and were in turn saluted by the trio.

After that Jack again started the engine, and they began moving with the current at a lively rate.

"Well, that was a new experience, now!" exclaimed Josh; "and we are mighty lucky to have escaped being taken back to Budapest and shut up in a dungeon."

"Yes, it was easy, after all," grumbled George; "but who'd think Hungarian officers would know English so well?"

"And just to think of our being taken for a lot of desperate Serbian youths sworn to get the aged and benevolent Emperor Francis Joseph! Ugh! it'll give me a shiver every time I think of it. I never dreamed before that I looked like a fellow who would take his life in his hand to do such a terrible thing."

CHAPTER V

SIGNS OF COMING TROUBLE

All day long the powerboat kept constantly moving down the reaches of the Danube River. Many were the interesting sights the boys looked upon from time to time. Nor did they see any particular signs of overhanging trouble. War may have been declared by Austria-Hungary upon Serbia and Russia, backing up the action of her ally, Germany, but the indications of it were not immediately apparent.

It was true that in several towns which they passed on that morning's run they could see that groups were in the streets, and there seemed to be many men in uniform hurrying this way or that. Once they also saw a field battery of glistening guns disappearing up a steep road that led to the south.

"You can see what's in the wind, all right," Josh remarked, as they watched a group of uniformed horsemen galloping along the river road as though bound for some distant point of mobilization. "In a few days after the call to the colors, as they say, has gone out for many classes of reserves, the whole country will be swarming with men in uniform."

"I only wish we could hold over and see what goes on," grumbled George. "It's a chance in a lifetime to be a looker-on in a foreign country, with war breaking out; and I think it's a shame that we are going to miss it."

Jack took him to task for saying that.

"We ought to thank our lucky stars, on the other hand, George," was the way he put it, "that we have a chance to get out of Austria before every exit is closed. I wouldn't be surprised if a lot of tourists have the time of their lives escaping, because, you see, every train will be taken over by the Government for carrying soldiers, guns, ammunition, horses, stores and such army necessities."

"Yes," added Buster, "that's what I say, Jack. For one I want to tell you I'm mighty thankful to be on board this old boat right now. I only hope they won't want to commandeer it for carrying soldiers down to the Serbian border."

"Oh, they wouldn't want to bother with such a mosquito craft as this, I should think," remarked Josh uneasily.

"Our little flag seems to attract a heap of attention," Buster continued, with a vein of pride in his voice, for that small edition of Old Glory was his private possession, it may be remembered.

"Where we landed at noon to see if we could buy some eggs and milk at that farm house," Josh observed, "those peasant girls were examining it. I rather think they must have somebody over in our country, for when I said the word 'America' and pointed to the flag and then myself they laughed and nodded their heads."

"And don't forget to mention, please, George, that we got the eggs all right," suggested Buster; "likewise a bumper mug of fresh milk apiece, and some butter that didn't have a bit of salt in it, which I think queer."

"Oh, so far as that goes," explained Jack, "there's lots of that made and sold over here. They call it sweet butter, and most people like it. You'd get used to it in time."

"Four dozen eggs, and whoppers at that," Buster went on to say, gloatingly; "which I consider a splendid investment; and we didn't have to pay half what they'd cost us in the States either. I'm going to have a couple fried for my supper, and anybody else that likes them that way can get what they want by giving the tip now."

They continued to chatter in this manner as the afternoon wore away. It had been decided that while there was a full moon that night they had better not attempt navigating the river after the sun had set. None of them knew what they might run up against; and besides, since war had come, possibly there would be strict rules enforced prohibiting such a thing during the night. None of them felt like taking chances.

Buster, it seems, must have been thinking of some of his previous exploits in the times that were gone, for later on he was seen to be looking over some fishing tackle he produced from his pack.

"Hey! what's in the wind now, Buster?" sang out Josh upon discovering what the fat chum was doing.

"Oh, nothing much," replied the other easily, "only it struck me that there might be some kind of eatable fish in this same blue Danube, and I'm looking over my lines. To-night, if I can find any fat grubs or worms, I might set a line and see what happens. You know I've had more or less success about grabbing big fish out of fresh and salt water."

That seemed to make the others laugh, as though certain humorous memories were refreshed. Buster joined them, for he was a jolly fellow and could even enjoy a joke when it was on himself.

"I mean to drop one of these lines over as we go along, so as to soak the snell of the hook, for if it's too dry it might break," Buster explained.

"Well, here's wishing that you meet with good luck," said Josh, "because I'd enjoy a supper of fresh fish pretty good."

"Don't make up your mouth for it, then," warned George, "because you never can tell about such things. Fish are what some people would call notionate; they bite well one day and then given you the grand laugh the next one."

"About how far do you think we've come since leaving Budapest, Jack?" Buster asked, not deigning to continue the discussion with George.

"I should think something like fifty to sixty miles," was the reply.

"Whew! as much as that?" whiffed George.

"Well, this current must be all of four miles an hour, and the old boat when going with it ought to average ten. Counting for our stops and all that, we've certainly covered sixty miles if we have one."

"I agree with you, Jack," said Josh; "George is only saying that to be contrary."

"Oh, I am, eh?" grinned George, who seemed to take especial delight in stirring Josh up.

"It's been a pretty good day for August, with the sun shining overhead most of the time, and not so very hot at that," Buster continued. "There's no sign of such a thing as a storm that I can see—great guns! what in the mischief can that queer-looking thing be over yonder? Do they have birds shaped like a fat cigar in the Danube country?"

Of course, every one immediately twisted his head around to take a look, and all sorts of exclamations announced that they were about as much astonished as Buster.

Low down toward the horizon they saw an object outlined against the sky that was undoubtedly moving, for they could notice that it passed a small cloud with considerable speed. Just as Buster had said, it looked very much in the distance like a fat cigar, and was of a neutral tint, not very easily distinguished against the heavens.

"Why, that must be one of those German Zeppelins we've read so much about!" exclaimed Jack, after taking a second look.

"A war dirigible, you mean, don't you?" demanded Josh.

"Nothing else," he was told. "I've seen pictures of them often, but never thought I'd set eyes on one. Yes, it's a Zeppelin, all right, and heading due south, too."

"What d'ye mean by saying that last?" asked Josh.

"Well, you remember what that officer said about the Serbians and Austrians on the Danube down below, where it acts as a boundary line, being ready to fight at the drop of the hat? Perhaps they're already having it hot and heavy. Perhaps the word has been flashed over the wires for one of the Zeppelins to come down and get busy there."

"What would they use it for, Jack?" questioned Buster, as all of them continued to watch the steady movement of the fast dirigible in the west.

"I believe the main thing for Zeppelins to do is to carry explosives and drop bombs from a great height on forts and barracks occupied by the enemy forces. But they can be also used for scouting and bringing back information of value. That may be what they want this one down along the Danube for."

So fast was the dirigible going that in a quarter of an hour more it had passed beyond the range of their vision.

"Looks like things are going to happen right along over in old Europe these days," remarked Josh.

"Yes, but we'll know next to nothing about it all," George went on to say; "for we can't buy a paper, and even if we did none of us could read Magyar. This thing of knocking around in a foreign country may be all very good when there's no war on, but there are times when you'd like to be able to buy an extra and learn all that's happening."

"There's a good landing by that tree yonder, Jack," remarked Josh.

"But we're not quite ready to pull in yet a while," the commodore announced.

"What's the hurry, Josh?" asked Buster, again working at his long and strong fish line.

"Oh, I thought George wanted to get out and start right away back," answered the other with a dry chuckle. "He'll never be happy until he can have all the comforts of home, including the afternoon extra to read."

"Forget it!" snapped George. "I've always been able to take things as they came as well as the next one, and I reckon I can stand what you fellows do. Because I grumble a little once in a great while, that's no sign I'm not having a good time. Some of my folks must have been sailors, I guess, and it runs in the blood. Don't pay any attention when you hear me complain."

"We'll try not to, George," promised Josh blithely; "we'll have to remember the source, and then forget it."

"There, now, I've got the silly old line untangled," announced Buster; "and I'll let the hook and sinker trail after us, just to make believe I'm fishing. It'll do me a heap of good to feel the twirl as the hook goes around with the swivel—sort of revive old memories like."

He lay there by the broad stern of the boat amusing himself after his fashion. Josh could not resist the temptation to warn him.

"Better look out for yourself, Buster," he remarked seriously. "Some hungry fish might snap at your bare hook and get caught. If you were taken off your guard the next thing you knew you'd be overboard."

"It wouldn't be the first time, either," mentioned George.

"Aw, no danger of that happening," retorted Buster good-naturedly. "Even over here in Austria-Hungary the fish have their eye-teeth cut, and wouldn't be so green as to bite at a bare hook. If I had anything to bait it with I'd watch my steps, you may be sure. But don't worry yourself about me, either of you. I can take care of myself."

No more was said just then with reference to the subject, something else coming up to catch their attention.

The afternoon was nearing its close, and Jack knew that before a great while they must be on the lookout for a place to haul up for the night. Whether they had better select a retired nook for their camp, as had been their habit when cruising down home rivers, or land near some farm, he had not yet decided. Of course, it would be unwise to stop over at any town, since they might have more or less trouble getting away again if the authorities chose to be exacting.

"There goes a long train over there, heading south, too," remarked Josh, pointing as he spoke.

"Seems like nearly everything is going the same way we are, for a fact," added George.

"It strikes me it must be a troop train," Jack was saying, "for, while I'm not dead sure, I think I can see men in uniform leaning from the windows of the carriages, as they call the cars over here."

"Well, what else could we expect?" Buster wanted to know. "If Austria means to give little Serbia a licking she'll need a lot of her soldiers down there, many more than she's got along the lower Danube now. Yes, they're soldiers, all right, Jack. I can see them plainly in the sunlight."

"The plot is thickening," remarked George solemnly; "and right now I wouldn't be surprised if the Germans were having a hot time over in

Belgium, if they've really started to cross the little kingdom. They say those Belgians are fighters to the backbone, and will never stand by to let the Kaiser cross their neutral country to strike at France."

George was deeply interested in all that was going on. He took pride in his knowledge of things connected with the aspirations of these countries, big and little, of Europe, and especially of the turbulent Balkan States. While George undoubtedly has his failings, as what boy has not, as a rule he seemed well informed, and could argue on almost any point.

"A lot of those fine chaps will like as not never come back," said Buster, as he gave the fish line another idle hitch around his wrist, preparatory to winding it in; "they start out full of enthusiasm and life, and are brought home again wrecks, fit for only the scrap heap."

"Listen to Buster, will you?" chuckled Josh; "he's getting to be a regular old philosopher these days."

"Well, it always did hurt me more or less when it came to parting with any one I cared for a heap," admitted the fat chum, trying to look serious, though that was always a difficult task with him, because nature had made his round features to bear the stamp of a jovial disposition; "you may remember that it took me two whole days to recover when we left home. I'm of a clinging nature, you see, and this thing of severing the bonds goes against my grain."

He had just said this when something happened that astounded the others. Buster seemed to be dragged from the end of the moving powerboat as though an octopus had suddenly flung one of its long tendrils up and clasped him.

The others heard Buster give one loud howl of fright, and then the sound was swallowed up in a splash as he disappeared in the river.

As Jack hastily stopped the engine and prepared to back up, he had a glimpse of the stout chum struggling desperately in the water. If his frantic actions counted for anything, it would seem as though Buster must be engaged in a life-and-death struggle with some marine monster that had pulled him from the after deck of the powerboat and into the river.

CHAPTER VI

THE CAMP ON THE RIVER BANK

"Keep a-going, Buster; we're coming back for you!" shrilled Josh, not a little alarmed on account of seeing such a tremendous splashing back where the stout chum was struggling in the river.

Being compelled to fight against the steady current, the boat could not make such very rapid progress, especially when backing up. Still it seemed as though Buster might be swimming toward them. He was using only one hand, and churning the water like the paddle-wheel of a Mississippi steamboat.

"Whew!" they heard him say, after ejecting a stream of water from his mouth, which he persisted in keeping open; "a sockdolager, I tell you! Going to beat all the records this time. It must be a river horse, or a boss sturgeon, boys. I want to save him, you bet!"

Evidently, like a true fisherman, Buster's first, last and only thought concerned the successful landing of the game he had struck. And presently the boat had come so close to the submerged boy that Jack stopped the engine lest the propeller do Buster some material damage.

Two of them leaned over the stern and with great difficulty managed to drag the water-soaked chum aboard.

"Sit there in the stern until you drain, Buster," ordered Jack. "If we took all that water aboard we'd be in danger of foundering."

"What ails your left hand?" demanded Josh.

"Why, don't you see," explained George, "the silly went and wound the line about his wrist. Then when the fish took hold it was a case of Buster going overboard or having his left arm pulled out of its socket. No wonder he lets it hang down like that now. I bet you it hurts like fun."

"But say, the bally old fish has quit pulling like mad!" exclaimed Buster, as though that circumstance troubled him much more than any bodily pain he might be enduring.

Josh leaned forward and took hold of the line. He even started to pull it in after the manner of a skillful fisherman, while Buster eyed him eagerly.

"Tell me you feel him pulling yet, Josh, can't you?" he pleaded. "Don't break my heart by saying he's gone! After all my fight I deserve to land that monster."

Josh chuckled.

"I do feel something now, all right, Buster," he remarked. "Watch me yank him alongside in a hurry. You never could handle such a monster with one of your arms next to useless."

So Josh worked away, possibly putting on more or less, as though he were having the time of his life in trying to drag the captive alongside. Every little while he pretended to lose a foot or so of line, whereupon Buster would call out anxiously and beg him to keep a tight hold on the glorious prize.

"Talk to me about having fish for supper," the dripping sportsman cried as he watched for the first glimpse of his catch; "why, we could feed a whole village on such a dandy as this. And caught on a bare hook, too! Ain't I the lucky one for keeps? What d'ye know about that?"

"There he comes, Buster!" cried Josh, pantingly; "get ready now to help me pull him up over the stern, all of you. My stars! but how he does fight."

In another moment Josh drew alongside a small but broad-nosed log, which in floating with the current of the river had suddenly been snagged by the bare hook. The impact, with the boat running as it was, had been severe enough to drag the fisherman into the water, for the stout line held, and he had foolishly wrapped one end of the same around his left wrist.

Jack and George shouted with mirth, and Josh excelled them both. Buster looked down at the now tamed "fish," felt ruefully of his lame arm, and then grinned.

"You bit, all right, fellows!" he blandly told them; nor would he offer any further explanation, so that to the end of the chapter none of them really knew whether Buster had been playing a trick on them or not by pretending to fight the object at the end of his line and showing such tremendous solicitude while Josh was pulling in the same.

"What am I going to do about drying off?" asked Buster a little later, after he had succeeded in reeling in all his line without getting it very much tangled—the log he allowed to float off on the current, having no use for it, though Josh did ask him if he had never heard of "planked fish."

"You're draining right along," George told him; "and as the weather is so nice and warm there's no danger of your taking cold, I guess."

"When we get ashore," Jack explained, "we can start a fire, and that will give you a chance to get dry. But I'm sorry about that arm, Buster. It may give you some trouble, because the jerk must have been fierce."

"Well, I should say it was," admitted the other, with a sigh. "I thought my arm would come off sure. But then the excitement kept me up, you see. And I knew right well you'd stop the boat and come back after me. But Jack, later on I want you to rub my arm with that liniment you carry with you. Chances are it'll be black and blue along the muscles. It hurts like fun even now."

Jack considered that the sooner this was done the better, so he turned the wheel over to George, and bidding Buster bare his arm, proceeded to give it a good rubbing with the liniment he knew to be fine for this purpose.

Buster was glad to find that as yet there were no signs of discoloration, as he had feared.

"It may last a few days," he cheerfully declared, "but that's the extent of the damage. I consider that I came off better than I deserved. But then, who'd think a bare hook would catch anything?"

"Well, Buster," warned George, "be sure you don't fasten your fishline to your leg, or around your neck. You never can tell what's going to happen; and after you're drowned it's no time to be sorry."

"I think we'd better go ashore below, where the trees come down to the edge of the bank," suggested Jack just then, showing that all this while he had been keeping a sharp lookout ahead.

"It makes me think of places where we've pulled up over along the old Mississippi," said Josh; "I wonder now do they have tramps over here, who prowl around looking for a chance to steal what they can lay hands on."

"I don't believe they do," George told him; "for they regulate such things a lot better than we do over the big water. Tramps are a luxury here, while with us they flourish like the green bay tree; the woods are full of them."

Jack took the boat in closer to the shore. On seeing the proposed landing place at closer quarters all of them seemed to be of the same opinion. It looked like just the camping ground they were looking for. A fire might be built for cooking purposes, and the district seemed lonely enough to make it appear that they might not be disturbed during their short stay of a single night.

On the following morning they expected to be once more on the move down the long and sinuous stream that covered hundreds of miles before emptying its clear water into the Black Sea.

As soon as the landing was effected Buster waddled clumsily ashore.

"I hope somebody will have the kindness now to get that blaze started right away," he was saying; "I'd do it myself, but I'm afraid all the matches I had in my pocket must have been soaked, and they wouldn't light easy."

"I'll take care of the fire, and do the cooking tonight in the bargain if you want me to, Buster," Josh told him.

"That's kind of you, Josh, and I won't forget it in a hurry, either. Fact is this arm of mine pains a little too much for me to sling the pots and skillets around in my customary way. But fry me two eggs, remember, Josh; I'd say three if nobody kicked up any sort of a row."

"You shall have them, Buster," Josh told him; "because the chances are we can pick up as many as we want as we go along."

"But no fish for supper tonight, how's that?" George demanded, trying to frown at Buster.

"Oh, well, nobody really promised you any," the latter explained. "But if there are any fat grubs in some of those rotten stumps around here I'm meaning to have a line out with three hooks to-night, and mebbe, George, you can indulge in fresh fish for breakfast. Will that do?"

"Guess I'll have to make it; besides, ham and eggs suits my taste well enough this time. I'll forgive you, Buster, only be careful not to get our mouths watering for fish again when it's only a floating log you've caught."

Josh was already busy with the fire. He had long since graduated in this department of woodcraft, and knew about all there was going in connection with fires of every description.

Then, too, he could cook in a way to make the mouths of his chums fairly water. Josh had a way of browning things so cleverly that they were unusually attractive, where so many boys more careless would frequently burn whatever they had on the fire, and in a happy-go-lucky fashion dub it "pot-luck."

"One thing sure," said Jack, as they sat around waiting for the call to supper, "we're a lucky set to have two such willing workers with the pots and pans as Buster and Josh here."

"That's right," declared George, agreeable for once; "it would be hard to find their match, search where you will. What one lacks the other makes up for, and the opposite way around too. And we want them to know we appreciate their services, don't we, Jack?"

"Come, now, no taffy, George," said Josh, though his eyes sparkled under praise from such a source; "as they used to say in olden days, beware the Greeks who come bearing gifts. And when you get to praising anything there must be a deep motive back of it."

"There is," assented George frankly, "a very deep motive, for I'm hollow all the way down to my heels, seems like. Sure the grub must be done by now, Josh. That's a good fellow, ring the bell for us to gather round."

Whenever these lads were sitting about the camp fire they always had plenty of fun on tap. If "jabs" were given at times it was done with such good-natured chaff that no one could get provoked.

So they started to discuss the supper Josh had prepared. Meanwhile Buster had managed to dry himself after a fashion by turning around near the fire, presenting first one side and then another to the heat. He likened himself to a roast fowl on the spit, and jokingly asked the others how they would have him served.

"After I'm all through eating my share of the excellent mess Josh here has provided for us," Buster remarked, when his mouth chanced to be empty, which was not often, by the way, "I know what I mean to do."

"Oh, anybody can guess that the first shot out of the locker," George asserted; "that is if they know what a fellow you are for remembering things. Of course you mean to smash some of these rotten stumps, and find out if they contain any grubs. Stumps are fine for holding the same, I understand; at least over where we live; and I guess grubs are grubs the world over."

"Yes, that's what I'm aiming to do," Buster admitted. "Just because I had the hard luck to be dragged overboard by a measly old log, don't think I'm the one to be scared off. If there are any fish in this Danube River, and they like bait such as I can offer them, we're bound to have a mess for breakfast."

"Hurrah! That's the ticket!" cried Josh; "if at first you don't succeed try, try again. I plainly perceive that my honors as boss fisherman are going to be put in peril if this thing keeps on. I'll sure have to get out a line myself, and run you a race, Buster."

"Wish you would," snapped the other, as though this just suited him.

"You remember," continued Josh, "we had some pretty tall rivalry in that line once or twice before. Never mind who came out first best; that's ancient history, and pretty musty by now. You find enough worms and I'll get a rig ready, Buster."

George rubbed his hands as though the prospect looked pretty bright to him. With two ardent anglers engaged in a warm contest to see who could do the better in the way of making captures, those who loved fresh fish might expect to be well taken care of.

When the supper had been disposed of, and every one declared he felt "full to the brim," Buster secured the little camp hatchet they had been wise enough to fetch along with them, and which had been a useful adjunct on many past outings.

With this in hand he started to attack some of the old stumps that could be seen scattered around. Josh felt considerable interest in his labors, as from time to time he could be heard calling out, and asking what the score was.

"Got three dandies in that stump," Buster presently made answer, "and here's a whole nest of bigger ones than the others. Say, we're fixed all right, my friend, so far as plenty of attractive bait goes. I can see a lovely time among the finny tribes when some of these fat boys get in the drink. They'll actually fight among themselves for a chance to bite; especially if you spit on your hook after impaling the grub."

By the time he had placed a full dozen of the victims of his hunt in the little can that had contained sardines at one time, Buster pronounced himself ready to begin serious operations.

Josh had in the meantime managed to get his line ready just as Buster finished his work; George told him it looked suspiciously as though he had been "soldiering," and meant to let his rival do all the work; but gallant Buster, hearing all this talk, immediately came to the rescue.

"And why shouldn't Josh take it easy, after going to all the trouble to prepare that fine supper?" he demanded. "You've got a bad habit, George, of looking a gift horse in the mouth, and the sooner you break yourself of it the better. Now, come along Josh, and let's find a good place for throwing our lines out into the river."

"We're not going to be partial or play favorites," warned Jack, laughingly; "may the best man win; but please don't try to give us any more planked shad, Buster, you hear!"

CHAPTER VII

WHEN THE STORM CAME

As Buster had taken a survey of the situation before darkness came along, he knew of a promising point close at hand. Here they could toss their lines out, and let the current drag them partly down-stream.

It was not the kind of fishing that the boys preferred, because they were accustomed to using jointed rods, and even casting artificial flies with which to lure the frisky trout or the hard-pulling black bass to their destruction. But as Buster wisely declared, "When you're fish hungry you've just got to shut your eyes and get 'em any old way; results are what count then, not methods."

Presently Buster had a savage bite, and drew in a squirming victim. He eyed this in the light of the rising moon and then remarked:

"I don't know the species that fellow belongs to, but he looks good to me, and all I hope is there are a lot of his uncles and his cousins and his aunts hanging around, anxious for grub bait. Hello! Got one, have you, Josh? Bully for you! Whew! He's a scrapper in the bargain, I tell you. I hope he doesn't break loose, and give us the grand laugh!"

Buster's interest was so taken up with what was going on near him that he forgot his own line for the time being, until a quick summons at the other end announced that one of the said finny relations seemed anxious to follow the first victim to the shore.

Then both boys were kept busy pulling in hand over hand. They succeeded in landing both prizes, which fact made them very joyful.

"Only needs one more to complete the first circle, though I think I'd like two for my share, Josh, and so might all the rest. You see there's a heap of waste when you come to take off the head and tail. Let's hurry up and get 'em while the bitin's good. You never can tell when fish will quit takin' hold."

It was certainly less than half an hour after they first started off when the two sportsmen came strolling back to the bright camp fire dangling a pretty string of still lively fish between them on a little pole.

"Two apiece, and one left for luck!" announced Buster, triumphantly, as the other fellows jumped to their feet with expressions of pleasure to look the catch over.

"They ought to be cleaned right away, and a little salt rubbed inside so they'll keep nice and fresh over night," said Josh, "so let's get busy, Buster."

"But don't you think that ought to be our part of the business?" asked George, although there was not very much animation in his manner, for George hated to handle the job of cleaning fish, though when it came to eating them no one ever knew him to make any objection.

"Now that's kind of you, George, to offer to do the thing for us," observed Buster, sweetly; "especially since we know how you detest the job. Thank you, but as our hands are in, Josh and me can attend to them all right."

Josh, however, did not look overly well pleased when he heard Buster say this. Truth to tell, he had already arranged it in his wicked heart that George should be trapped into "doing something for his keep."

"We'll let you off this time, George," he remarked, pointedly, "but the very next batch of fish we haul in you can tackle the job."

George only chuckled, and drew a sigh of relief. Perhaps he may have said to himself that sometimes people count their chickens before they are hatched, and that possibly there might never be another "batch;" remembering the story of the small boy who while eating an apple, upon being appealed to by an envious comrade to give him the core, told him "there ain't a-goin' to be any core, Jimmy."

In due time the fish were laid away in a safe place where no roving animal was apt to discover and appropriate them. Buster might in his happy-go-lucky fashion have been careless in this particular, but shrewd Josh was far too smart to take unnecessary chances.

"We don't know anything about the country around here," he told the others. "They may have wild animals, and again p'raps there's nothing of the kind to be feared. But it's best to lock the stable before the horse is stolen."

So the fish were kept aboard the boat, although from time to time George might have been observed to sniff the air suggestively as he prepared to sleep, plainly indicating that he disliked the fishy smell. But then George always was what Josh called "finicky" in his habits, and the rest seemed to pay little or no attention to things that annoyed the particular one.

When morning came, without any untoward happening, Buster took particular pains to cook that mess of fish to a beautiful brown color. He followed the old and well known camp method of first throwing several slices of fat salt pork into the skillet and rendering it down. Then when it was boiling hot he placed as many of the fish as it would accommodate in the pan, first rolling them in cracker dust. Turning them back and forth as was necessary he finally had them looking so appetizing that the others refused to wait a minute longer, but made a raid on the lot.

The breakfast was a pronounced success. Even George was heard to say that he did not care how soon it was repeated; which was quite reckless on his part, since he had been given due warning as to his duties next time.

The sun was well up and shining brightly when they left the scene of their camp. It promised to be a rather warm day, Josh predicted, after taking a look around at the sky, and sizing up the breeze. Josh pretended to be something of a weather sharp, though hardly calling himself a prophet along those lines.

"And," said he, as they started down the river again, "it wouldn't surprise me a bit if we ran into a squall before we see that old sun go down tonight."

"Do you really mean that, Josh?" asked Buster.

"All humbug," muttered George, disdainfully, as though he never pinned any faith on "signs," and considered all weather predictions as founded on mere guess work.

Josh shrugged his shoulders as he went on to say:

"Oh! very well, just wait and see if I know beans or not, that's all. They have some pretty lively thunder storms along the Danube, I'm told, and if that's so what better time than in August could you expect to run across one? Course I may be mistaken, because I'm only a tenderfoot of a weather sharp; but wait and see."

"Oh! we will, Josh, we will," replied George, in his tantalizing way.

The morning passed pleasantly enough, though as noon came on it might be noticed that everybody showed signs of being hot. The sun certainly did blaze down upon them, and it was even warmer inside the cabin of the powerboat than outside, so it seemed useless trying to get any relief by seeking the shade.

They drew in at a place where there were trees, just to lie around for possibly an hour under their shelter, while they ate a cold "snack." It was too furiously hot to dream of building a fire and making a pot of coffee.

Then once again they embarked for another run down-stream. Jack figured they had covered more distance that morning by five miles than on the other day. This fact cheered them up immensely, and as they continued to go with the current they took their customary interest in what was to be seen along the eastern shore, where they would not have the bright rays of the declining sun in their eyes.

Many were the odd sights they beheld from time to time. First it was this thing that attracted them, and hardly had their exclamations of delight ceased than something else would be discovered further down that chained their attention until they were close enough to make out its character.

One thing Jack called their attention to, and this was the fact that they were meeting with more evidences of mobilization than ever, as they proceeded further from the Hungarian capital.

The news may have been belated in reaching many of these interior hamlets and pretty little towns along the Danube; but it must have arrived at last, and no end of excitement had followed.

They saw scores and even hundreds of men in uniform, some marching in squads as if hurrying to join the colors; others guarding bridges, or other vulnerable structures, the latter doubtless being old men who could not go to the front, though still possessing the military spirit, and desirous of doing something for the country of his birth.

Jack was delighted with this chance to see things he had often read about but never really expected to set eyes on.

"I used to believe that it was a terrible crime to have every young fellow serve a couple of years in the army before he could go into business, and then be reckoned as belonging to the reserves, but I'm changing my mind some, let me tell you," was what he said later in the afternoon.

"How's that, Jack?" asked Buster.

"Well," continued the other, obligingly, "in the first place it makes for a love for their country when they know they represent a unit in her defense. Then again it goes to make the young fellows amenable to discipline, something millions of boys in our country are lacking in. It teaches them to be frugal, and the life outdoors makes them a lot more healthy."

"Sounds good to me, Jack," assented Josh.

"I know we've done a heap of talking over in America about the mad folly of Germany in making every young man serve a term in the army, and boasted that our boys needn't ever fear of being forced to join the colors; but perhaps, fellows, after this world war is over, we'll be doing the same thing. Preparedness is what is going to count for a whole lot, let me tell you; and both Great Britain and the States will learn a lesson before they're through."

At the time of course Jack was only taking a vague peep into the future; but events that have happened since then show he had a wise head on his young shoulders. When these words are being penned camps are springing up all over the States where business men can have a month's training in military ways; and those who come back home admit that they have taken on a new lease of life, such are the great benefits to be obtained in that fashion.

It must have been past the middle of the hot afternoon, when the boys were lolling about, almost panting for breath, and taking things as easy as possible, that a sudden sound startled them.

"Thunder!" ejaculated Buster, as he popped up his head to look around.

Black clouds were sweeping swiftly down back of them, and even as they looked a flash of vivid lighting resembling a forked dagger shot toward the earth, almost immediately succeeded by another deep-toned burst of thunder.

"What do you say to that, George?" demanded Josh, turning a triumphant face on the other.

"Oh! seems like you hit the mark with that guess," admitted the other, "but then anybody might one out of three. Besides, we haven't got the storm yet, have we? It may go around us."

"No danger of that," declared Josh; "these summer storms nearly always follow the channel of a river. I've known 'em to pour down pitchforks for half an hour on the water and the other bank, and never a drop fall on me. But we'll get all the rain you want to see right soon now."

"I do hope it'll cool the air some then," complained Buster, who being stouter than any of his chums, must have suffered more in proportion from the heat.

"What had we better do, Jack?" asked George, surveying the black clouds uneasily.

"It's too bad that we don't happen to see any cove where we could run in and stay," replied the pilot; "so on the whole I think we'd better make a turn and head into the storm that's coming down the river."

"That sounds good to me!" declared Josh, instantly understanding the benefit such a course would likely bring to them; "our cabin is partly open in the rear, but well protected forward. We can use that tarpaulin to cover the well back here, and after all the storm won't last long. Swing her around, Jack, and edge in a bit closer to the shore while you're about it. The river is pretty wide right here."

It seemed three times as wide to Buster just then, as at any time before; but of course this came from his suddenly awakened fears.

"How deep do you think it can be out here, Josh?" he asked after another fearful rolling crash of thunder had passed into rumblings in the distance.

"Oh! a mile or so," replied Josh, carelessly.

"Whee! then all I hope is we don't get blown over on our beam-ends, and have to swim for it," Buster was heard to say.

They had just managed to get the boat headed up-stream when the squall struck them with almost hurricane force. The water was lifted and flung against the little boat with terrific violence. Indeed, the boys working energetically could hardly manage to fasten the stout tarpaulin to the hooks by which it was meant to be secured in an emergency like this, so as to cover the open well at the stern.

The rain began to come down in wild gusts, the wind howled around them, the boat rose and fell frantically, and Jack had all he could do to keep the plunging craft headed into the furious storm.

It grew almost dark around them. Water found entrance despite the cover, and the boys prepared to take a soaking. As they were not made of salt, and had undergone many privations and discomforts during other days, they uttered no complaint. Indeed, Buster was telling himself that it would be all right if they only got through in safety; clothes could be easily dried, but it was another thing to be wrecked out on a raging river in a storm like this.

The waves were mounting pretty high, so that with every plunge they could tell that the propeller was fighting the air, as it was hoisted above the resisting water. This was what alarmed Jack, for he knew the danger attending such a sudden and constant change of speed.

He tried the best he could to ease the strain each time they rose and fell; but it was always with an anxious heart that he listened to hear if the propeller still continued to do its duty after every mad plunge.

Minutes had passed, just how long a time since the beginning of the storm none of the boys could tell. Then all at once every one noticed that they had ceased to progress steadily. The noise of the churning propeller had also ceased.

"We're turning broadside to the blow, Jack!" shouted Buster, although that was hardly the case as yet, his fears magnifying the danger.

"What happened, Jack?" roared Josh.

"Engine's broken down, and we're at the mercy of the storm!" came the staggering reply.

CHAPTER VIII

THE SPORT OF THE ELEMENTS

"Just what I expected!" exclaimed George, when he heard what Jack had to say.

"Will the boat upset, do you think?" bellowed Buster, as he fancied he could feel the craft already tilting dangerously, so that he "sidled" across to the other side of the crowded little cabin.

"Oh! I hardly think it'll be as bad as that," the commodore told him; "but while we're about it we'd better fasten on these life preservers!"

They had discovered half a dozen cork belts under one of the lockers, and these Jack proceeded to hastily throw out. Every fellow was immediately engaged in trying to buckle one about his person, well up under the arms.

The thunder bellowed at quick intervals, so that talking could only be indulged in between these outbursts. It was almost dark inside the cabin of the rocking boat, and of course the boys were all very much excited, not knowing what was going to happen at the next minute.

"Be sure to get it up under your arms, Buster," warned Jack, while he worked.

"Yes," added Josh, who could be sarcastic even when confronted by such danger, "for if the old thing slips down any it'll keep your feet out, and your head under water. Better put two more on you, Buster, because you're a heavyweight, you know."

Perhaps Josh was joking when he said this, but Buster took it all solemnly enough.

"Guess I will, if the rest of you don't need 'em!" he declared. "If you're done fixin' yours Josh, please lend me a hand. I don't seem able to get the fastening the right way. Oh! we nearly went over that time, didn't we?"

"Keep still, Buster, and quit trying to balance the boat!" urged George; "your weight won't matter a bean if she's bound to turn turtle; and you nearly smashed my foot that time, you came down on it so hard. Talk to me about a sportive elephant, it isn't in the same class with you when you get excited."

"Here, I'll try and fix you up, Buster, if only you keep quiet a spell," Josh told him, and between the two mentors Buster resolved to bear up and show a brave front.

Jack was peeping out as if hoping to see some sign of the storm breaking. The boat meanwhile was wallowing dreadfully, showing that by degrees she must be turning sideways to the waves and the wind, the latter still blowing "great guns."

A vivid flash came just when Jack had the tarpaulin drawn aside, and made Buster give a loud cry.

"Oh, what a scorcher!" he exclaimed; "I thought I was struck at first."

The speedy crash that followed drowned the rest of his words.

"Any hope of its being over soon, Jack?" demanded Josh, as soon as he could make himself heard.

"Nothing doing that I could see," came the loud reply, for what with the howl of the wind and the dash of the agitated waters against the boat it was no easy matter to make oneself heard. "All black around. You can't see twenty feet away for the rain and the gloom."

"Jack, do you happen to know whether there's any rapids or falls along the Danube?" asked George presently.

"I'm not so sure about it," replied the other; "seems to me I did hear some talk about rapids or falls or something, though it may have been about the river away up above Vienna."

Buster at that found himself possessed with a new cause for alarm. He pictured Niagara Falls, and the powerboat plunging over the beetling brink, with four boys he knew full well fastened in its interior, helpless victims. Then as the mood changed he could see Whirlpool Rapids below the falls, through which no ordinary boat had been known to pass safely, but always emerged in splinters, after buffeting the half-hidden sharp-pointed rocks, and urged on by the frightful current.

"Listen! I thought I heard a distant roaring sound just then that might be the falls, fellows!" Buster broke out with.

Although the others all suspected that it was only the result of a lively imagination that caused him to say this, at the same time they could not help straining their hearing to ascertain whether there could be any truth in it.

"You fooled yourself that time, Buster," announced George finally, and with a vein of positive relief in his voice; "it must have been the rain coming down like a cloud-burst, or else the wind tearing through some trees ashore."

The action of the boat continued to cause more or less anxiety. Frequently when the wind struck savagely on the counter of the wallowing craft it would careen over so far that even Jack feared a catastrophe was impending.

Everything conspired to cause alarm—the darkness, the heavy crash of thunder, the blinding flashes of lightning that stabbed the gloom so suddenly, and the possibility of the boat turning turtle.

In the midst of this Jack was seen to be crawling out of the cover.

"What are you going to do?" shouted Josh.

"All of us have forgotten that we've got an anchor forward," Jack told him; "I'm going to drop it over. It may take hold; and anyway it's bound to keep our head into the storm by dragging!"

"Let me help you, Jack!" added Josh with his usual impulsiveness.

"You may come along, but no one else," he was told.

Of course, that was aimed primarily at Buster, for Jack could not forget how clumsy the fat chum always proved himself to be; and the chances were that he would manage to fall overboard did he attempt to crawl along the slippery sloping deck.

Once outside and Josh realized what a difficult thing it was going to be to get forward to where the anchor might be found. The little boat rolled and tossed like a chip on the angry seas. Josh felt almost dizzy with the motion, but he shut his teeth grimly together and resolved to stick it out to the end. If Jack could stand it surely he should be able to do the same. Besides, he would sooner die almost than let George see him show the white feather.

"Get a good hold before you move each time," called Jack in his ear; "and better grab me if you find yourself going!"

That was just like Jack's generous nature; he thought nothing of the added risk he was assuming when he gave Josh this advice.

Josh would never be apt to forget that exciting experience as long as he lived. Except when the lightning came it was as impossible to see anything as though they were in the midst of a dark night; and even then all they could detect was what seemed to be a wall of gray fog enveloping them on every side, with the white-capped waves leaping and tossing like hungry wolves around them.

Of course, both boys were immediately drenched, but of this they thought nothing. Both had their coats off at the time, on account of the afternoon heat, which turned out to be a lucky thing for them, since their movements were apt to be less fettered and confined in consequence.

Foot by foot they made their way forward. Jack's advice to always retain one grip until the other hand could take hold of something ahead saved Josh more than once from being thrown overboard. A little recklessness would have cost him dear in a case like that.

Finally Jack seemed to have gained his end, for he was bending down over the anchor when a flash of lightning enabled the other boy to see him again. Josh, determined to have a hand in casting the mudhook overboard, hastened to join him.

"The end of the cable is fast all right, is it, Jack?" he shouted, as together they took hold of the rusty iron anchor.

"Yes. I made sure of that before we started, and tested the cable in the bargain," he was instantly assured.

It was a good thing some one had been so careful, for Josh himself had evidently not given the matter a single thought.

"Look out not to get a leg tangled in the rope, Josh!" shouted Jack.

"I will, all right!" the other replied, knowing that in such an event he would be dragged overboard like a flash.

So the anchor was let go.

There was no result until the whole of the cable had been paid out. Jack waited anxiously to see what followed, though he knew fairly well it would steady the drifting boat and turn the bow into the storm again.

Both of them felt the sudden jerk that announced the expected event.

"She's turning right away, Jack!" bellowed Josh, trying to make himself heard above the heavy boom of the thunder's growl.

There could be no doubt on that score, for already the motions of the runaway motorboat seemed to be much less violent. Jack believed his scheme was going to be a success, and it pleased him to know that his wetting would not have been taken for nothing.

They lingered no longer, but started back toward the stern. It was not quite so difficult now to creep along the slippery deck, holding on to the cabin roof, and finally reaching the open well in the stern. A head was in sight, showing that one of the anxious chums could not rest easy until he learned what the result of the venture had been.

"You must have done it, fellows!" exclaimed Buster, for it was no other than the stout boy who had thrust his head out like a tortoise, "because she rides so much easier now. I knew Jack'd manage it if anybody could."

Drenched as they were, the two boys had to drop down under the tarpaulin. After all, that was a minor matter, since by their bold action they had warded off what might have turned out to be a grave disaster.

"Let her blow and thunder all she wants to now," said Josh triumphantly; "we've got the anchor trailing from the bow, and that's going to keep her nose in the wind. I've read how a vessel nearly going down in a hurricane has been saved by making a storm anchor out of hatches, or anything else that will float, and towing the same behind to keep the ship steady. That's what we did, you see."

Josh was more than glad now he had insisted on accompanying the commodore in attempting to carry out his hazardous undertaking. It would give him an opportunity to swell with importance whenever the deed was mentioned, and to use the magical word "we" in speaking of the adventure. What boy is there who does not like to feel that he personally partook of the danger when brave things were undertaken and accomplished?

After that they settled down to wait. The storm must surely come to an end before a great while, and as they were now moving at less than one-half the mad pace they had been going before that drag had been instituted, it seemed perfectly safe even to Buster.

"All I hope for now is that we don't run afoul of some half-sunken rock, or it may be a snag!" Josh was heard to say.

"We do know there are snags floating along, because you remember I struck one only yesterday," ventured Buster, referring, of course, to the log which, by catching his trailing fish hook, had dragged him overboard.

"Not much danger of that," Jack assured them; "they keep a pretty clear channel over here, it seems, even if we haven't met steamboats on the river like you would on the Mississippi. Given another ten minutes or so and I think we'll see the break in the storm we expect. It can hardly last much longer now."

"Must have done some damage ashore, too, boys?" suggested George.

"So long as it hasn't killed off all the chickens, so we can't get any more eggs, that doesn't really concern us, I s'pose," said Buster, not meaning to be unfeeling in the least, but just then that seemed to be in the nature of a calamity in his mind.

Slowly the time passed, but the boys were soon delighted to discover that there was actually a slackening up of the elements that had combined to make such a furious discord. The thunder became less boisterous, the wind lulled perceptibly, and even the waves had lost much of their force.

Jack, taking an observation, made an important discovery, and followed it with an announcement that gave his comrades considerable pleasure.

"There's a break in the storm clouds over there in the west, boys, and I guess we've got to the end of this trouble!"

"With no damage done except a wetting for two of us," added Josh, trying to act as though that counted for next to nothing, considering the benefits that had probably sprung from the work of Jack and himself.

"Why, it seems to me the rain has let up, too, Jack!" exclaimed Buster, forcing his head through the opening in the tarpaulin cover of the well.

"In a few minutes more we can get rid of this old thing and breathe free once more," Jack told him.

"Well, I'm sure I'll be mighty glad," said Buster, "because I'm nearly stewed as it is, with the heat below here; and that breeze feels mighty good to me. It won't be near as warm after this storm, that's sure."

"Like as not, Buster," advised Josh, shivering a little because of his wet condition, "we'll all be frozen stiff before an hour goes by. Queer things happen over in this Danube country, I'm told."

"Rats! You can't scare me, Josh," Buster immediately informed him; "course, since you're all wet through and through you might freeze, but not a healthy specimen like me. This time we'll have to make a fire for you other fellows, if we can find enough dry wood to burn, that is."

Jack's prediction was soon fulfilled. The break in the storm clouds grew rapidly in magnitude until quite a large sized patch of blue sky became visible. They soon had the tarpaulin dragged on top of the cabin roof to dry out; and when the sun appeared the pair who had been drenched took positive delight in sprawling there and letting the warm rays start drying their garments on them.

"Well, seems like we got through that scrape O. K.," ventured Buster; "but we're not yet out of the woods by a big lot. We've got a broken engine on our hands, and no means of fixing the same, even if we knew how to do it. What's to be done now, Commodore Jack?"

Somehow the others always thought to give Jack his full title when relying on him to get them out of a scrape. But Jack let this significant fact pass, for he knew these three chums from the ground up, and could not hold a single thing against any one of them. And, as usual, he had a remedy ready for every disease.

CHAPTER IX

THE HUNGARIAN MOB

"There's only one thing we can do," Jack told them, "which is to work the boat along closer to the western shore. Before long, unless my map of the river is all wrong, we ought to strike a town by the name of Mohaca, a railroad place situated on a sharp bend of the Danube, and there must be some one in that town who can do the necessary repairs to our engine, if we hold over half a day."

The others admitted that the plan proposed by their leader sounded good to them. And accordingly they set to work first of all to get the trailing anchor aboard, so that their progress would be delayed no longer.

Buster was much relieved. Besides, it was Josh who was saturated to the skin now, and when one means to be cheerful it counts for considerable "whose ox is gored," as Buster liked to put it.

Still he felt sorry when he saw Josh shivering, for the air had become suddenly quite cool after the passing of the storm, and insisted on wrapping a blanket about the slim boy.

All of them kept watch for signs of the town below. The afternoon was wearing on very fast now, and they hoped to arrive before sunset. It might be a difficult matter to find the machinist they wanted if they reached the town on the bank of the Danube after darkness had set in.

"I reckon it's at that bend below there," said Jack; "if you look sharp you can see the sun glinting from what looks to me like a church steeple, with a cross on the same."

"You hit it that time, Jack," asserted Josh, "because that's just what it is. For one I'll be glad to get where we can have a fire and dry out."

They were compelled to work pretty hard in order to get the boat over close to the shore where the town stood. The current seemed to run in a contrary direction, and did its best to frustrate their efforts.

Jack, however, remembering many other times when they had been aboard motorboats that acted queerly, or else broke down, had seen to it that there was a push-pole lashed to the side of the craft. The river at this point proved to be comparatively shallow, so that it was easily possible to reach bottom.

By changing hands, and each one having a turn, they kept where they wanted to go, and in this way made the town.

It did not differ from other places they had been seeing along the Danube, and after the storm it looked rather subdued. In the morning they would find the customary amount of life in the place, together with the usual display of soldiers' uniforms, Jack did not doubt in the least.

As they were passing slowly along in search of some place where they might hope to have their broken-down engine repaired on the following day, as well as a harbor of refuge for the coming night, loud cheers drew their attention to the railroad which ran close to the river bank.

"It's only another train-load of troops going to the front!" announced Josh, as they saw numerous heads thrust from the windows of the carriages, together with wildly waving hands.

"They think it's a picnic to start with," said George, "but before long they'll sing a different tune, I guess; that is, those who live through the first battle. In these days of quick-firing guns and the terrible shells, the chances a fellow has of coming back home are mighty small. No soldiering for me if I know myself."

"Oh, that's all hot air you're giving us, George," scoffed Josh. "You know mighty well that if our country was in danger, and you were old enough, you'd enlist right away. So would we all of us, as well as Herb and Andy at home. You've got your faults, George, as all of us have, but being a coward isn't one of them by a long shot."

George did not make any reply to this speech, but smiled as though he felt rather pleased to know even Josh had such a good opinion of his fighting abilities.

The long train with its shouting crowds passed from sight. Evidently these troops were headed for the Servian border, and expected to see warm service there, fighting against the brave little country that had long since won its independence from the Turks.

"I think I see what we're wanting to find," remarked Jack presently.

"It's the usual boatyard you find in nearly all river towns," added Josh; "and we ought to be able to make arrangements for having our engine looked over and repaired in the morning."

"Make your minds easy on that score," advised George, calmly enough; "for even if we don't run across a machinist who can do the job, trust me to tackle it."

"What! you?" ejaculated Buster.

"Why not?" demanded George, as though aggrieved that any one should for a moment question his ability in that line. "Haven't I taken the engine of my Wireless to pieces many a time and put it together again?"

"That's right, you have," spoke up Josh, "because you never could let well enough alone, but must be monkeying around your engine all the time. That's why Jack insisted in the beginning of this voyage that you were to be a passenger and let him act as pilot and engineer."

"But the engine's broken down, isn't it?" demanded George.

"Sure it has," Josh admitted, "but that was a sheer accident, and you didn't have a thing to do with it."

"There's no reason to believe we'll get left about finding a machinist here," Jack remarked, to calm the troubled waters. "I think that sign tells us as much. But we'll soon know."

They managed to push the boat inside the enclosure. Here they found a number of river craft of various types, and Jack noticed that among them were several launches, from which fact he judged that the man did all kinds of general repairing.

A short time later they landed and found the owner of the shop. He could understand English, fortunately enough, so they were able to make a bargain with him. Doubtless he must have charged them an exorbitant price, for upon their accepting his terms he showed them unusual courtesy, even telling them to push the boat inside his house, where he could get to work at the engine in the morning.

He also informed the boys that if they chose to sleep aboard they were at perfect liberty to do so. Should it storm again they would have the benefit of a roof over their heads; and they could cook their supper at the fire he would leave in the forge.

Buster immediately declared it would be a jolly thing all around.

"You know we do feel more or less cramped aboard our boat," he went on to remark, with considerable eagerness. "And if you say the word, why, I'll take my blanket and camp out here on the floor. There are plenty of chips to make a soft bed, even if they don't smell as sweet as hemlock browse such as we have at home."

"And another thing," added Josh, "Jack and myself can get nice and dry at the fire here in the forge. I think the man must have noticed that we'd been soaked."

"Yes, and he soaked us some more in the bargain," complained George, "according to the price we agreed to pay him for the easy job of mending a broken engine. See, you might have saved all that money if you'd had enough confidence in me to let me run the job."

"Perhaps!" said Josh dryly, and there was such a world of meaning in that one word as pronounced by him that George immediately fell silent, not caring to bring about another verbal controversy.

The owner of the boatyard and shop was certainly very kind in allowing those who were perfect strangers to him to remain over night there. He must have seen by looking at the faces of the four boys that they were worthy of trust. It was not everybody whom he would grant such a favor to, and Jack told his chums they had reason to feel quite proud of the fact.

It was by this time getting quite dark. The man had lighted a lamp for them, which served to dispel the gloom in the shop's interior. Josh was already using the bellows in order to blow the dying fire into new life. When the heat became noticeable he and Jack proceeded to warm up. By degrees they found that this steaming process dried their clothes admirably. Buster could tell them how efficient it had been in his own case, only that Buster was now impatient for them to get through, so he could have the red bed of coals for the purpose of cooking supper.

At the time the proprietor of the boatyard went away Jack had stepped outside the door with him. As he expected, he found that the shop faced on a street running close to the river itself.

As they had laid in plenty of provisions at Budapest, there was really no necessity for any of them to wander around the town. If the boys exhibited any curiosity in that respect, Jack meant to dampen their zeal by telling them there might be some danger of strangers being eyed with suspicion in these exciting days, and that it would be safest to stay at the shop.

Besides, there could be no telling just when the repairs would be finished, for, after all, the damage was apt to be slight; and in this event they would want to be on the move with as little delay as possible.

Bumpus was soon in his glory. It had indeed been a long while since they had enjoyed the privilege of preparing a meal over such a fine fire as the blacksmith forge afforded them. Besides, the glowing coals seemed so much nicer than ordinary smoking wood; as Bumpus said, it saved the cook's back considerable, in that he did not have to bend down so much.

They found something that answered for a table, and by the light of the lamp so kindly loaned by the owner they ate their supper. No matter what it consisted of, for there is no time to go into particulars—at least it had a "homey" taste to it, and brought back to their minds numerous other meals which had accompanied their various cruises down American rivers, through the Great Lakes, and among the islands of the Florida coast.

It seemed very quiet down by the river. If the town itself was booming with the spirit of war, the boys heard very little of it while they sat around chatting, after partaking of the meal Bumpus provided.

Once George sauntered over to the door that led to the street and looked out, but he did not venture forth. When he came back Josh, of course, wanted to know what he had heard.

"Oh, nothing much," the other replied with a yawn. "There's considerable noise up above, and perhaps some soldiers are getting ready to go away. You know they make an awful lot of fuss over here when the boys are off for the war."

"So far as that goes, they do it everywhere," remarked Jack. "I remember plainly hearing my folks telling all that happened in our town in ninety-eight, when the war with Spain broke out. Of course, all of us were kids then, babies in fact, and we knew nothing about it; but I take it there were lots of exciting things happening day after day, as trains passed through. One country doesn't differ a great deal from another, when you come to take notice."

"I hope you took pains to put up that stout bar again, George, after you shut the double doors?" remarked Bumpus. "Not that I expect we'll be troubled with unwelcome visitors in the shape of thieves while we're roosting here, but you know it's a heap nicer to know everything's lovely and the goose hangs high."

"Oh, don't borrow any trouble about that bar, Buster," George assured him. "Sure I put it back, just like I found it. I reckon the owner uses it when he's working in here behind closed doors and doesn't want to be disturbed. You know he locked the small door before going away. It's all right, Buster, so let your dear timid soul rest in peace."

"Oh, not that I'm afraid," asserted the other indignantly; "honest, George, I only mentioned the matter as a simple precaution. Jack here might have done the same, given a little more time. You ought to know me better than that, George."

The boat lay tied up in the basin inside the shed. Back of it was a water gate, which had also been closed and fastened by the owner before departing. Surrounded as they were by all the tools of a boat repairer's trade, the boys felt as though they were in strange company. Possibly some of these same tools were built along different lines from what they might have found in the same sort of an establishment in the States.

For quite some time the four chums sat there and talked over various things of interest. Of course, these as a general rule had some connection with their own fortunes. Many questions were asked and answered, by one or another, as the case might be, although as a rule it was Jack to whom most of them were addressed. The whole scheme of a cruise down the Danube had originated with Jack, and for this reason, as well as others, the remaining three boys looked to him to find answers to the many puzzling enigmas that faced them.

Jack was fully qualified to assume this task, and it was seldom they were ever able to "stump" him with a twister.

So the time passed on, and, judging from the repeated way in which some of the motorboat boys were yawning without even putting up a hand to hide the gap, it became evident that they could not remain awake much longer.

Indeed, Jack himself felt pretty drowsy, and was just about to propose that the meeting adjourn sine die, so that each could prepare his cot for the night, just as he saw fit, when something occurred to interfere with this peaceful scheme.

"Listen! Seems to me that hollerin's coming closer to us," exclaimed Josh.

"Sure it is," added George, which was pretty conclusive evidence pointing that way, because as a rule he would have questioned it before giving in.

"There's a crowd coming," said Jack quietly.

"More like an angry mob, it sounds to me," muttered Josh.

"Say, you don't think for a minute, do you," cried Buster, "that they know about us being hidden in this coop, and mean to interview the bunch, perhaps shoot us for Servian spies?"

"Oh, hardly as bad as that," Jack went on to say, seeking to calm the excited Buster; "they may pass by and never bother us at all. Perhaps some soldiers are going along to a place of meeting, where they expect to entrain for the front."

"Anyway, we'll soon know the worst," declared Josh, "because they're nearly up to the shop by now."

The shouts outside had an angry and insistent ring about them that Jack did not like. Then came a series of heavy and imperative knocks on the closed shop doors!

CHAPTER X

CLEVERLY DONE

"My stars! it's us they're after, fellows!" Buster was heard to gurgle, when the knocks ceased as suddenly as they had begun.

No one had to be told that, for they all knew it just as well as Buster. George turned an anxious look on Josh; and then, perhaps unconsciously placing their hopes on their leader, both of them wheeled to face Jack.

"I knew we'd be sorry if ever we tried stopping over at one of these ratty little towns," muttered George.

"But there they start to knocking again!" exclaimed Josh. "If we don't do something, and pretty quick at that, they'll start to pulling this shanty down over our heads, even if it is made of stones."

Jack had to think fast. He knew Josh spoke the truth, and that so far as offering resistance went they were practically helpless against the mob. He could easily imagine how in some manner suspicion had been excited against the four young strangers stopping over night at the river town. One word would lead to another in these exciting times, until all sorts of extravagant surmises must result; and finally some bold spirit must have suggested that they proceed to the boathouse and drag the unknown parties out, to question, perhaps hang them.

So far as trying to escape was concerned, it seemed equally hopeless. Besides the double door there was also the small one, which the proprietor had securely locked before leaving them. Both led to the street.

To be sure, there were the water gates, but to leave in that way must necessitate abandoning their motorboat, something the boys would be loth to do. Further than this, there was no small boat handy, even if they could manage to get it out on the river without being noticed and pursued.

As to attempting to swim off, that was impossible, since they could not make any headway with their clothes on, and leaving these behind was not to be considered for a minute.

So Jack quickly decided that the only thing left for them was to throw open the double doors and trust to their customary good luck to make friends with the clamorous mob without.

"I'm going to open up, fellows," he told the others. "You keep back of me, and say nothing unless I ask you to speak. Leave it all to me to manage."

"You just bet we will, Jack," assented Josh.

"I should say yes," Buster hastily added.

"It's a risky thing to do, Jack," remarked George, "but seems that we haven't got much of a choice. We're between the devil and the deep sea. Go ahead, then, and let's see how our luck holds good."

Jack waited no longer. Indeed, it would have been dangerous to have held the clamorous crowd in waiting much longer, for their pounding on the door had assumed a more threatening phase, several having taken it upon themselves to pick up heavy stones, with which they started to beat the woodwork furiously, while all manner of loud cries arose.

Suddenly the double doors were swung wide open. The outcries ceased as if by magic. Jack, looking out, saw that fully fifty people stood in the moonlit street. Most of them were men and boys, though a sprinkling of women could also be seen.

They were typical Hungarians, just such people as one would expect to meet in a river town along the lower Danube. Some were flourishing what appeared to be clubs, and the whole aspect of the mob looked threatening indeed.

It required considerable nerve to calmly face this crowd, but Jack actually smiled, and waved his hand in friendly greeting, while Buster held his breath in very awe, and the other two trembled a little between excitement and alarm.

One burly man in the front of the mob called out harshly. Jack could not for a certainty know what he said, but it was easy to guess he must be demanding who they were, where they came from, and what they were doing in this part of the country in these perilous times.

So Jack, waving his hand to entreat silence, called out:

"Is there any one here who can talk English!"

Somehow his question created considerable surprise. Evidently the crowd had suspected that they were Serbians or natives of Montenegro, both of which states at the time were antagonistic to Austria-Hungary.

Several voices were heard announcing that they could understand and speak the English language. Jack swept his eyes around to see who these persons were, and, discovering that one of them stood in the front rank of the crowd, he pointed at the man as he went on to say:

"Please push your way up here. We will tell you everything you want to know, and you can explain to your friends."

The man did so, looking very important. Perhaps that was the first time in all his life that he had been called upon to act in such a capacity as interpreter, and he felt as though placed upon a pedestal.

"Now, if you will please give me a chance, all of you," continued Jack, "I will with the greatest pleasure tell everything. In the first place, we are not, as you think, English boys, but Americans. Of course, you know about America, for we have many thousands of good Hungarians over there working with us, who send millions on millions of dollars back home every year for the old folks. Tell them what I have just said, will you?"

The man had listened intently. He collected his wits, and then, turning around so as to face the rest, commenced speaking. At the same time he made good use of both hands, in the Hungarian fashion, to emphasize his points.

Some few of the more unruly made remarks among themselves as he proceeded, but on the whole the crowd listened intently. It was already apparent to Jack that he had gone about the business in the right way, and had succeeded in making a good impression.

He had read recently in a paper, whether it were true or not, that the tens of thousands of Hungarians in the United States, men in the mines and working on public improvements, and girls in service, sent back home during the course of a year as much as a hundred and fifty million dollars. Even if a third of that amount came across the sea it could be understood that the people of the dual monarchy must have a very tender spot in their hearts for America, where so many of their compatriots were making big wages and happy.

"Keep it moving, Jack," whispered Josh. "I tell you they're already on the run. Lay it on thick, and don't spare the adjectives. They like to hear things praised up to the skies. And say something nice about old Francis Joseph, because, you know, they worship him."

"Cut it out, Josh," growled George; "leave Jack alone to run this game, can't you?"

The man had by now finished telling what Jack had said to him. He again turned with a look of expectancy on his face, waiting for the second "installment of the story," as Josh afterwards called it.

"We are American boys," continued Jack, "who have come over here on a vacation. In our own country we own three motorboats, with which we often cruise up and down the Mississippi River and others. So, having heard so much about your beautiful blue Danube, we made up our minds to spend a month or six weeks voyaging down it. This boat does not belong to us. We hired it from a man in a town part-way between Vienna and Budapest. We can show you the paper both parties signed proving how we paid a certain sum in advance for the use of it until we reached the Black Sea. Now tell them all that, please, while I get our American passports ready to show you, as well as letters we have received from our home while in Budapest."

It took the interpreter a long time to translate all this. He struggled heroically to master every detail, though Jack feared he might get mixed more or less in his endeavor to find words to express the English meaning.

The crowd listened intently.

It would have been amusing to watch their faces as seen in the bright moonlight had the danger element been lacking. As it was, the boys were still on the anxious seat, not knowing "which way the cat would jump."

Jack was the exception, it may be said. He felt that his tactics and the frank way he was taking the crowd into his confidence had already made a favorable impression upon most of the men. They in turn would be apt to suppress any of the more boisterous spirits who might feel like getting out of bounds.

Truth to tell, it was as much the manner of Jack Stormways as what he said that worked this change in the feelings of the populace. No one of intelligence could very well look upon his smiling face and believe ill of him.

By the time the man had managed to translate all that second batch of explanations to his fellows Jack was ready for him again. He had meanwhile collected from the other three their passports, properly vised through the efforts of the American consul in Vienna, and also several letters addressed to the general delivery at Budapest, with the American stamps and postmarks to prove where they had come from.

These papers he now handed to the man who could speak and read English. Each one Jack opened and explained, after asking Josh to fetch the lamp forward so that its light could be utilized.

Meanwhile the crowd listened and pushed and gaped, some exchanging low comments; but Buster was delighted to see that the threatening gestures had stopped. From this he felt that Stormways' stock was rising fast and would soon bull the market.

It took a long time to go over the four passports with their seals, and then read extracts from the letters. The man spoke several times, asking questions, which proved that he meant to conduct his examination in a thorough manner. Jack was in truth pleased to find that he had to deal with so intelligent a party, for the travelers had really nothing to conceal.

He even mentioned about the three Hungarian officers who had overtaken them some miles below Budapest, coming in a speed launch, and how they had parted the best of friends after looking the boys over.

Seeing that the crowd was becoming impatient, Jack cut his explanations short and asked that the interpreter make his report to his friends. He had taken the advice of shrewd Josh, and managed to speak highly of the aged emperor; while this may have been done artfully as a stroke of diplomacy, Jack really knew nothing but good of Francis Joseph, of whom he had often read, so that he did not feel that he was attempting any deception.

Still holding the sheaf of passports, the man started to harangue the crowd. He seemed to improve as he gained new confidence, and Jack saw that he was something of a crude born orator, able to sway others by the force of his will and words.

Jack believed the best part of their luck lay in having picked on this particular man. Another might have bungled things and made them worse than they were originally.

It took a very long time to explain about the papers, the letters and everything else. Jack even heard the man mention the emperor's name, and from this judged that he was repeating what the boy had said in order to prove that the four strangers from America were favorable to the Austrian side of the controversy.

"He's got 'em whipped to a standstill, Jack," muttered Josh in the ear of the other. "They'll do whatever he tells 'em, you mark me. I guess I can read all the signs if I can't understand the lingo."

Jack himself believed the same thing. He no longer felt his heart heavy within him, with the prospect of having their fine cruise broken off and themselves thrown into some prison, from which it would take all the efforts of the American Ambassador to release them.

Before the man who was speaking had finished there were desertions from the mob, possibly some of those more ardent spirits who had hoped to help hang a suspected Serbian spy and were grievously disappointed.

When the speaker closed with what seemed to be a fervent peroration there followed a general shout and much waving of hands. Jack caught the one word America, and judged that the cheers were intended for his native land, for surely many of these people had good reason to think of the haven of the oppressed as a Paradise flowing with gold, milk and honey.

Then the mob began to disintegrate. A number who could speak English came crowding around. They wished to shake hands with the four stout-hearted lads who were not to be deterred from continuing their hazardous voyage down the Danube by the mere fact that hostilities had begun, and that there must be heavy firing between the Austrian batteries and monitors and the hostile forces in Belgrade, the Serbian capital, situated on the southern bank of the river.

By degrees they went away, after giving this popular demonstration. Somehow Buster changed his mind completely after seeing how those same shouting men could turn into friends. He even remarked afterwards that he thought the Hungarians were a warm-hearted race, and that he was growing to like them immensely; though when he first saw the mob he believed they were a lot of cutthroats eager for the lives of helpless American boys.

The interpreter was the last to go. Jack was seen to shake hands heartily with him for the third time ere saying good-by.

"I reckon now, Jack," remarked George, as they closed the double doors once more, shutting out the bright moonlight, "you slipped a bill of some kind in that fine fellow's hand the last time you said good-by to him?"

"Never mind about that, George," retorted the other; "if I did, that's between the two of us, and nobody need know about it. It was worth ten times as much just to see the way he swayed that crowd. From howling at us they came to cheer us, and a good deal of the change was due to his oratory."

"As for me," piped up Buster, with a great sigh of relief, "I never will forget this experience. There was a time at first when I thought of having my head put on a pike and carried in a procession around town, just like the mob used to do in the French Revolution; or, if it wasn't that, I expected they'd get a rope and swing us all up, Wild Western way. I tell you I'm shaking yet from being so anxious about you fellows."

Josh and George laughed at hearing this, and the whole of them went back to their seats.

CHAPTER XI

UNDER FIRE ON THE RIVER

Later on the four boys made themselves as comfortable as the conditions allowed, and tried to settle down for the night. Buster had carried out his words, and managed to gather enough shavings to make a soft bed on the floor, using his blanket to cover the same. Josh imitated his example, but the others were satisfied to occupy their old places in the boat.

None of them slept soundly, and for good reasons. The recent excitement made such an impression on their minds that they could not for a long time stop thinking about the visit of the mob.

Then again there was always the chance that some of the wilder spirits might think they had been cheated out of some fun, and come back in the small hours of the night to renew the trouble.

Several times, when some sound was heard that at another time would hardly have been noticed, one or more of the seeming sleepers would raise his head to listen, proving that sleep had been remote at the time. Buster in particular was uneasy, and even after he managed to get asleep Josh declared he tossed about and muttered to himself at a fierce rate.

But, after all, their fears proved groundless. The townspeople had accepted them at their face value, and did not mean to bother the strangers again. No one came prowling around the boatshop during the balance of the night; and with the arrival of dawn the boys were all up, ready to cook breakfast and clear the shop so that the proprietor could get busy.

They had a simple meal, only coffee, boiled eggs and buttered toast; but every one ate all he wished, so there was no complaints coming.

Then came the owner of the boatyard and shop, who was greatly surprised when he learned what had happened on the preceding night. He seemed indignant at first, but calmed down when he heard how the mob had changed from enemies into friends after finding that the boys were from America.

He told Jack that he could give a surmise as to what had prompted the attack. Strangely enough, it concerned that story of the four desperate young Serbians who, according to accounts, were said to have started for Vienna with the avowed intention of depriving Austria-Hungary of their beloved old emperor, just as some other wild spirits had murdered the heir apparent and his wife.

Apparently this story was believed by all who heard it. Those Serbians were getting very bold of late, and nothing seemed to be beyond them. They were also earning the mortal hatred of the Hungarians, Jack could see.

When the assistant worker arrived the two of them began to overhaul the engine of the powerboat. George stood around every minute of the time and watched, as well as asked innumerable questions. The others, however, made him promise not to offer to render the least assistance. They knew George's failings, and feared that if he once got to pottering with that engine it was surely doomed.

Apparently the man knew his business thoroughly. Jack, after seeing how he went at matters, felt sure the trouble would soon be located and remedied, when they might go on their way rejoicing.

It was about ten o'clock when the engine was started up and responded handsomely. Buster gave a whoop of delight, while Josh swung his hat above his head, and the others also smiled in satisfaction.

"Everything is lovely and the goose hangs high!" Josh announced, as he jumped up and chinned himself against a handy rafter of the low shed.

"We can all see that without your telling us, Josh," George chuckled.

Of course, every one was in a fine humor now. Their stop had not proven so serious after all, since they had only lost a few hours. As to the sum asked by the machinist, that did not bother them at all, since there was plenty more where that money came from.

As there was now nothing to delay them, they said good-by to their friend of the boatyard and were soon moving down the river again, delighted at their good fortune.

"Another odd experience, that's all," sang Josh, as they took their last look back at the town on the point before turning another bend that would hide it entirely from view.

"But at one time, I tell you, it promised to be pretty serious," Buster asserted. "We've got one asset, though, that never fails us."

"What's that?" asked George.

"The Stormways luck!" laughed the fat chum. "In fair weather and foul, and through storm and stress it can always be depended on to bridge over all difficulties and drag us out of every old mud-hole or swamp. If you look back to our past career you'll find that what I'm telling you is nothing but the honest truth. It's better to be born lucky than rich any day."

Jack only laughed at hearing this. He knew that luck alone is rather a flimsy foundation to pin confidence on, and that there is something more needed; but it was not for him to say as much. If his comrades believed it all a matter of accident, they were welcome to the delusion.

Somehow they enjoyed the sensation of freedom more than ever on this day. Perhaps that came from the unpleasant experience of the preceding night, when they found themselves in danger from the angry mob.

It was not long before Josh broke out in song and amused himself for a spell, entertaining his chums as well, for he had a pretty good voice. When they were passing through a hilly region, with rather abrupt walls on either shore, it was a peculiar experience that befell them.

"Somebody's mocking you, Josh!" cried Buster indignantly, when they all heard a voice distinctly repeat the last few words of the song Josh had finished.

Jack smiled to see the other three look hastily around, for he guessed the secret immediately.

"Try again, Josh, and see if he keeps it up," he went on to say, and when once more the same mocking call came back to them Josh began to grow quite "huffy."

"Think yourself smart, don't you?" he shouted, shaking his fist toward that point from whence it seemed the taunting voice hailed.

"Smart, don't you!" came immediately back at him.

Then Buster must have seen a great light, for he gave a loud laugh.

"Say, don't feel like hitting him, Josh, because it's only an echo!" he gurgled.

"Don't you believe it!" snapped George. "No echo could ever repeat words as plain as that."

"Try it yourself and see, George," advised Jack, and, realizing that he was in a poor minority, George did give a shout, only to have it sent back with an abruptness and energy that startled him.

The doubter was apparently convinced, though he kept saying that he never would have believed it possible for an echo to repeat such things. As they were speeding along with the current they quickly passed beyond the magic range, and hence Buster received no answer when he shouted lustily at the rocky hillside.

As they had lost so much time that morning, it was decided not to make any stop at noon. They could manage on some cold lunch, and wait until night came along to do their cooking.

They frequently saw other boats on the river. Many of these were clumsy affairs and evidently owned by farmers, who were in the habit of getting their produce to market in this way. Occasionally they passed a small pleasure boat loaded with people, who, like most excursionists, waved their hands and handkerchiefs at the four comely lads aboard the chugging motorboat.

Seeing Jack, who had temporarily handed the wheel over to George, examining his little chart of the river, procured in Vienna, Josh came and dropped down beside him.

As usual, Josh bristled with interrogation points. He came of Yankee ancestry and never could pick up enough information to satisfy himself. There was always a yearning to "know" whenever Josh came around, and he would go straight to the heart of the matter without any beating about the bush.

"Making pretty good time, eh, Jack?" he went on to say as a prelude.

"Splendid, Josh, and I'm thinking that overhauling is going to pay us fairly well in the end. It certainly has increased the speed capacity of the boat by a mile an hour, according to my reckoning."

"Bully for that!" ejaculated the other; "and provided we keep this same pace up for five or six hours more, whereabouts do you think we might stop over night?"

Jack must have been doing a little figuring along those same lines himself, for as Josh leaned over he put the point of his lead pencil close to a cross he had made on the chart further along.

"Providing all goes well, that's about where we ought to fetch up on this day's run," he told Josh.

"Looks like we might get to the Serbian border then by another night, eh, Jack?"

"That's possible, unless we have another accident, or get held up some way or other. While we may figure as much as we please, it's never wise to count your chickens, Josh, before the eggs are hatched. There's always a big IF confronting us, because we're doing this thing under peculiar conditions, you know."

"By that I suppose you mean the plagued old war that had to break out just when we got well started on our way?" complained Josh.

From one subject he launched into another, until he had pumped Jack dry—at least the other laughingly told him so as he scrambled to his feet, after replacing his chart in his pocket, and went over to relieve George.

The long afternoon was wearing away, and so far everything seemed to be going on all right. Buster called attention to this fact every little while, as though it occupied a prominent place in his mind.

He even allowed himself to remember that he had promised to try and duplicate his fishing feat and supply the party with a change in breakfast food.

"Josh," he went on to say, "are you game to run another race this evening with the balance of our grubs? They've kept alive all right, and ought to be good for a mess of fine fish."

"I'm your meal ticket," cheerily announced the other. "Count me in the game if the chance opens up; and I hope we have as good luck as that other time. But say, there's a queer looking boat away down the river that I don't seem to be able to make head or tail of. Somebody take a look and tell me what you think."

At that there was a general craning of necks. Then Buster announced his opinion.

"Whatever she is, I think they're anchored in the stream, because I can't see any movement at all."

"But that looks like smoke coming from a stack of some sort," George observed, as he cupped both hands in order to shield his eyes from the bright sunlight, in this way securing better results.

"Strikes me it's a cheese box on a raft of some sort," Josh gave as a hazard.

"Why, Josh, that was the name the Confederates gave the Monitor in our civil war, you know," burst out Buster; "the single round turret was built on a low deck just a little above the water, and I suppose it did look like a cheese box, such as you can see in the grocery stores at home."

"Between you," said Jack just then, "you've guessed it."

"Do you mean it's really and truly a monitor?" demanded George skeptically.

"I've understood that Austria had a number of these river gunboats down here, and I think they all mount pretty big guns, as well as being armored," Jack went on to say.

"But what use would they be?" queried George.

"Well, you must know that this eternal Balkan question is forever bobbing up, and within a few years there have been two serious clashes south of Austria. The first was between Bulgaria, Serbia and Greece against Turkey. They knocked the Sultan's forces out and took a lot of territory away, which they divided. Then Bulgaria got a notion she could lick the other two and seize more territory; but the shoe was on the other foot, because she had to cry for quarter, and lost a good portion of land that had come to her from Turkey. Ever since there has been bad blood between them all, Rumania also."

"But how does Austria come in with their petty quarrels?" continued George.

"Do you remember the old fable of the lion and the bear fighting over the game they had taken until they were exhausted, and then the sly fox walking off with it? Well, Austria got hold of a monstrous slice of territory in something the same way—Bosnia and Herzegovina. And there's a big scheme afoot, I believe, for the Teuton allies to take Serbia and unite the German-speaking countries with Turkey."

"Oh, I remember reading that Germany had eyes for Persia and all that rich Eastern country," admitted Josh.

"Well, they are figuring on great things out that way," Jack continued. "As for these river monitors, they are here to threaten little Serbia with. You see, it's unfortunate that the capital, Belgrade, lies just across from Austrian heights, and always in reach of hostile batteries."

"Shucks! that was foolish of the Serbians," said Josh disdainfully, after the manner of one who knew it all. "Long ago they should have moved their capital to Nisch, nearer the middle of the state. Then they could defend it a heap better."

As they approached closer to the singular craft anchored there near the shore of the river the boys eyed it curiously. They could see many men aboard, doubtless the crew. There was also an officer using a pair of binoculars, for they could catch the gleam of the sunlight on the glasses as he moved his hands.

Without the slightest warning, when they were almost opposite the anchored monitor, there came a puff of smoke and a reverberating boom. The boys saw the water splash high in the air about twenty feet in front of their little boat, showing that it had not been blank shot after all.

Buster was at once in a panic. He really believed that in another moment they might be the target for one of those big guns that could be seen projecting from the movable turret aboard the monitor, and at that close range the result must be the total annihilation of boat and passengers.

CHAPTER XII

NEARING THE SCENE OF WAR

"Pull up, Jack; that's a plain invitation to hold our horses!" shrilled Josh, being the first one to find his voice.

Jack already knew this. He shut off power and then started to reverse, for the impetus of the craft, not to mention the swift current, was carrying the boat forward at a good pace, and any sign of disobeying that naval summons might cost them dear.

"There, he's beckoning to us to run over alongside," said Josh. "Mebbe we'll be given a chance now to see what one of these same river monitors look like."

"Huh! like as not we'll be given a chance to see what a musty old dungeon under some Austrian fortress looks like!"

Of course, it was George who made this last gloomy prediction; but then the others were so accustomed to his ways that no one paid the least attention to him.

Jack was already heading the boat toward the anchored vessel. All of them had a very good chance to observe what a monitor looked like as they approached, and if they failed to accept their opportunity, that was their fault.

Coming up from below, they bumped against the armored side of the bulky war vessel. Buster looked with something of awe at the gaping guns of large caliber that projected from the turret close by.

When Josh, coached by Jack, had tossed a rope to some of the waiting crew of the monitor, they prepared to go aboard. Jack might have limited the number to himself and perhaps Josh, but then he knew the others would always be sorry they had not been given the privilege of saying they had once been aboard a fighting warship while war was on; so he allowed both George and Buster to trip after.

It could be seen that the officer was plainly surprised when he saw them at close quarters. Instead of the local boys whom he might have expected to meet, he now realized that the tiny flag floating from the stern of the motorboat stood for something.

"Who are you, and where do you come from?" he asked in excellent English, doubtless realizing that it was useless to ply them with Magyar.

"We are American boys, sir, as you can see from our flag," Jack told him. "It is the only one we happen to have along with us."

He thought that the captain looked very much interested, and that his manner became immediately a shade more cordial, which proved that he knew considerable about the country across the ocean.

"But this is a strange place for four American boys to be taking a cruise, you must admit," he told Jack.

That gave the boy a chance to begin explanations. He went over the same ground as before and told how as members of a motorboat club they had planned to voyage down the Danube, and only learned of war breaking out when on the way.

When he mentioned the matter of passports the officer indicated that he should like to see them, at which once more Jack called upon his chums to produce their papers.

"You will find them all correct, sir," he assured the other; "and besides, here are some letters from home which we received from our folks. They reached us in Budapest, you can see. I would like you to glance over them so that you may know we are just what we claim to be."

The officer seemed to be pretty well satisfied after he had examined the passports. At the same time he looked at the boys in an amused fashion.

"Which one of you is George Rollins?" he asked, somewhat to the astonishment of that worthy, who did not know what might be in store for him, honors or captivity.

"That's my name, sir," he spoke up, and, to the further surprise of the boys, the Austrian commander thrust out his hand.

"I want to shake hands with you, George," he said.

"Y-yes, sir," replied the other, still groping in the dark, and fearing that he might be perilously near the edge of a precipice.

"You wonder why I single you out from your companions," continued the other, as George accepted his hand and received a cordial squeeze in return. "I'll have to explain, I suppose. Did you ever hear your mother speak of a cousin who had married an Austrian gentleman many years ago?"

Then George found his tongue.

"Oh, yes, I certainly have heard her speak of her cousin Lucy, and the name of the gentleman she married was—let me see, Stanislaus!"

As George burst out triumphantly with this declaration he found his hand once more shaken and squeezed, while the commander of the monitor beamed upon him.

"Well, I am Captain Stanislaus, and my mother was that same Cousin Lucy you have heard about. So you see, my boy, we are kin. I am very glad to meet you, even under such singular conditions."

George turned toward his companions. His face was one broad smile. He doubtless had a pretty good sense of his own importance just then.

"I want to introduce my three chums to you, Cousin Stanislaus," he went on to say with an air of importance. "The one you have been talking with is Jack Stormways, our leader; the stout one is Buster Longfellow, and the other is Josh Purdue, all of them the finest fellows under the sun, and my pards."

The officer gravely shook hands with each of the boys in turn. He seemed to be duly impressed with the recommendation given by his newly discovered relative.

"See, here is a letter from my mother, sir," continued George impulsively and with a deep motive back of his actions. "Her name is Alice, and she is first cousin to your mother. How pleased she will be to learn that I ran across you in this remarkable way! And because we are related, as it seems, I hope you will allow us to continue our voyage down the river, for it would be a great disappointment all around if we had to give it up now."

Jack felt like clapping George on the back when he heard that naive appeal. Evidently George believed in making use of his relatives. What was the use of blood ties if favors could not be obtained through them?

All of them waited anxiously to see what the commander of the monitor might say. Ties of relationship might be all very well, but there was such a thing as duty to the Government to be considered. Of course, he knew very well that nothing was to be feared from these American boys, who would not have any reason for carrying news to the hostile Serbians. Hence it was really only a matter of their taking unnecessary risks in trying to pass the disputed portions of the Danube where opposing batteries might be bombarding each other.

The officer looked from one to another. He saw only appealing glances that undoubtedly must have made him weaken in his first resolve to order the boys back and end their adventurous voyage then and there.

"We are accustomed to looking out for ourselves, believe me, sir," Jack thought fit to say just then, hoping to be able to influence the commander, who seemed to be what Josh would call "on the fence."

"All we expect to do," George went on to say, "is to slip past some night when it happens to be cloudy, and, once by the Iron Gate, the way is clear for us on to the mouth of the Danube. We have spent a heap of money to have this trip, and it would break us all up if we had to quit."

The officer laughed at that.

"Well," he went on to say, "I suppose, after all, it is none of my business, and I could allow you to proceed without any risk that you would carry important news of troop movements to the enemy beyond the Danube. It is with regard to your mother, George, I am thinking most of all."

"Oh, don't you fear about her, sir!" cried the boy enthusiastically. "She knows I've always been able to paddle my own canoe and find some way to get out of every sort of scrape. Please say that you will wash your hands of us and let us go about our business."

"Very well, let it be just as you will have it, George. I do wash my hands of the whole business. You see, I have been young myself not very long back, and know what it means to a fellow to be terribly disappointed. Only promise me on your word of honor that you will not run any unnecessary risks in trying to pass Belgrade in the night time."

Of course, George was only too glad to do this, and so they were allowed to go aboard the motorboat again, parting from the Austrian commander with mutual wishes for good luck.

George was about the happiest fellow going during the next hour. He seemed to be beaming with good nature.

"Did you ever hear of such a remarkable thing happening in all your life?" he demanded of Buster, whom he had cornered. "To think that, with the whole of this big country of Austria-Hungary to choose from, we should have picked out the Danube River for our cruise, and that just at the same time my second cousin with his warship should be stationed down here! Then again, remember how he fired a shot across our bows to bring us to, and, seeing my name on my passport, realized that we were actually blood relations!"

"It was queer, for a fact," agreed Buster.

"Queer, you call it, do you, Buster?" cried George. "Why, I think it the most astonishing coincidence that ever happened. I'm sure none of us have even run across its equal. And then, what's more, he let us proceed just because I was his cousin twice removed. Don't forget that, Buster, will you, some time when you and Josh feel like giving me a dig or two? Oh, I'm of a little consequence once in a long time."

"You're of a whole lot of consequence plenty of times, George," said Josh just then, "and we all acknowledge the corn; but for goodness' sake please give us a change of tune now. We've been hearing about Cousin Stanislaus until even the swallows swinging past seem to be chirping the name; and I expect the fish will give it to us, too, if we catch any to-night."

George looked a little hurt in his feelings at this thrust, but he subsided all the same, going off by himself where he could ponder upon the freaks of fortune that had thrown him in contact with this relative at the other side of the world, so to speak. From time to time he would smile as though his thoughts were pleasant ones; but none of the others interrupted his meditations.

The day drew near a close, and as they had really come up to Jack's expectations it might be set down as possible that they would camp somewhere close by the place marked with a cross on the chart.

That would mean only one more day's journey before they must find themselves in the vicinity of battle scenes, if, as they suspected, the Austrians had started to bombard Belgrade and were being answered shot for shot from their fortifications by the valiant Serbian gunners.

They were fortunate enough to find a particularly good camp site. It was in the midst of some trees that offered them all the comforts they could wish for. At the same time they had no reason to believe they were anywhere near a town, and the river in this spot looked quite lonely and deserted; at least there was no other war monitor in sight, from the deck of which their movements might be observed and deemed suspicious enough to warrant a visit of investigation.

As evening drew on they tied the boat securely and built a fire close by. Buster, as usual, insisted on taking charge of the cooking, while the rest lay around or gathered fuel for the fire.

It was while moving about with this latter purpose in view that Jack suddenly came upon a crouching figure in the brush. At his exclamation the unknown party struggled to his feet. Jack had been alarmed at first, not knowing but what there might be bandits in that vicinity. He quickly saw, however, that he had a peaked looking and very hungry fairly well grown boy to deal with.

Not wishing to let the other see that he had been startled, Jack immediately demanded to know who he was and why he was spying on them. The other made motions to let Jack understand he could not speak English. He then went on to say something in rapid tones, but it was all Greek to Jack.

However, from his appearance and the motions he made to his mouth, as well as showing how empty his stomach was, it was easy to judge that it was the smell of the cooking supper that had drawn him.

"Stay with us, then, and share our meal," suggested Jack, mostly in pantomime; and evidently his gestures must have had a convincing way of their own, for the hungry boy immediately nodded his head, said something in a fervent tone, and, to Jack's embarrassment, proceeded to kiss his hand violently.

"Hey, what's all this going on here?" asked Josh, just then coming on the scene, no doubt attracted by the sound of a strange voice.

"Here's a poor tramp of a boy who gives me to understand he's half dead with hunger," Jack went on to explain; "and as we can't turn him away in that condition, we'll have to let him stay to supper with us, I suppose."

Josh, of course, was exceedingly surprised. He looked the strange boy over and saw that he undoubtedly had a hungry appearance.

"Sure we'll share our supper with him, Jack," he hastened to say, being one of those fellows who could never see any one suffer when he had a chance to offer assistance; "who knows but what we may be entertaining an angel unawares, like we read about. Tell him to come along up to the fire right away."

Buster and George were also somewhat astonished at this increase to their number. Still the poor chap looked so woebegone that Buster immediately saw to it that an extra portion of food was prepared. George, too, did not have the heart to show his objecting nature. He thought this to be a real case of necessity.

The strange boy was fairly well grown, though slender. His face was dark and he had a mass of heavy black hair. His eyes were dazzlingly bright, and, although there was an uneasy look on his face, he could smile cheerily when he saw that any of them were looking at him.

Josh watched him from time to time, as though some notion had come into that shrewd head of his. Supper was getting along nicely when Jack saw Josh beckoning to him cautiously at a time the stranger happened to be looking another way.

Then Josh strolled off a short distance and seemed to be bending down, as if looking at something that interested him.

"What's in the wind?" asked Jack softly, as he joined the other.

"I don't know exactly, to tell you the truth, but I'm uneasy over something, and wanted to have a little chin with you," came the reply.

"You're suspicious, that's what, Josh?"

"Oh, well, I admit as much," replied the other. "You see, in these times we've got to be careful. Instead of an angel we may be entertaining one of the other kind."

"Now get it out of your system, and tell me what you're thinking about," demanded Jack.

"First of all, he turns his head and looks every little while in a certain direction. I've got a good notion the boy must have friends hidden somewhere near by."

"Yes, go on, Josh; what else?"

"Then, if you come to think of it, he doesn't talk the same lingo as these Hungarian Magyars we've met. I'm not dead sure about it, but I've got a hunch he must be of another nationality. Well, what nation are we closest to below here? What but Serbia? Are you following me, Jack?"

"I am, so keep going," the other informed him.

"You remember the story we were told by that polite Hungarian officer, about the four desperate Serbian youths who had sworn to have the life of the aged Austrian emperor—well, according to my notion, our guest is one of the batch; and his three tough cronies are hidden close by, waiting for some signal!"

CHAPTER XIII

THE BOY FROM SERBIA

Jack remained silent for a full minute after his companion had delivered himself of this startling statement. He was evidently thinking it over. Perhaps up to then Jack had not even suspected the tramp of being anything more than he seemed, a well-grown lad who was far away from home—and hungry.

Presently Jack spoke again, and from his manner it became apparent that he now shared in some degree the alarm that Josh seemed to be laboring under. Really, the conditions were suspicious enough to demand an investigation. They were next to unarmed, and if four desperate young fellows raided their camp they would find it difficult indeed to keep from losing everything they possessed, from boat to supplies.

"I hate to think that such a thing can be possible, Josh," he said slowly, "but, as you were remarking, the circumstances force us to be on our guard. Before we start to eating supper, which must be nearly ready now, I'll try and strike up a conversation with the fellow and learn something about him."

"But how on earth can you do that, Jack, when neither of you seem able to understand one word of each other's tongue?"

"Oh, leave that to me, Josh. There are ways, you know, even if I have to come to paper and pencil and use the picture writing of the Indians. What with signs and nods and looks we may get a fair understanding."

"No harm trying, that's a fact," admitted Josh. "But I'll watch my chance and put the others wise. Every one of us ought to have some sort of club handy so as to protect the camp and the boat if there's going to be a raid."

Apparently the more Josh considered the subject the stronger became his belief that he had hit the truth in making that guess. In his eyes the dark face of the young stranger now began to assume a threatening appearance, whereas before it had only seemed hungry and eager and almost sad.

Jack watched his opportunity and soon found a chance to drop down beside the stranger. He saw that there was intelligence in the face of the other. It could also be seen in his flashing eyes. If Jack had only been able to understand and speak the other's language he felt sure he could induce him to tell his story.

He took out a pencil and a pad of paper and began to draw. As Jack was a master hand at this sort of thing, he quickly produced a sketch that represented four boys, all dressed alike, and in the costume which the young stranger wore.

This he held before the other, and then pointed to him as he nodded. After looking at the drawing intently the boy shook his head. It was evidently intended for a denial that he had three companions, but then Jack could hardly have expected him to admit it openly.

One thing sure, he did not seem to be alarmed, as though suspecting that his secret had been discovered; only puzzled.

As if governed by a sudden impulse, he motioned for the pencil and paper, just as Jack expected he would do, and in his turn began to draw something. When he handed the pad back it was seen that he had actually made a pretty accurate map of the enlarged Serbia of to-day; doubtless every schoolboy in that country was early taught to be able to do this, on account of the great pride the Serbian people took in their recent victories over Turkey and Bulgaria.

He had even written in bold letters the magical word "Serbia" across this map, as if determined to remove all doubt as to what it was meant for. Such frankness made Jack begin to believe that the other could not possibly be the desperate character Josh suspected; had he been, it would only have seemed natural for him to deny his nationality lest he be arrested and put in an Austrian dungeon.

Jack went a step further, after the boy, first pointing to his map, smote his own chest proudly and smiled, as if to proclaim that he belonged in that country. By various gestures he tried to ask the other what he was doing here in a hostile land.

The other watched his every gesture and seemed to be reading even the expression on Jack's face. It is surprising how much can be learned that way. Whole conversations may be carried on by instinct and intelligence. One who does not know a single word of Italian may be able to sense the general meaning of many paragraphs in a newspaper war item by the similarity of words. Try it, and you will see that this is really so.

By slow and laborious degrees Jack began to pick up something of what the other was trying to tell him. The further he proceeded the more intense did the boy seem to become. Buster, glancing that way from time to time, filled with curiosity, considered that they were using their hands almost as cleverly as a couple of mutes did whom he had once watched talking in the sign language.

Of course, Josh had before then managed to whisper to each of the other two what a "mare's nest" he believed he had unearthed, so that both George and Buster had begun to look on the intruder in the light of a dangerous fellow. George kept caressing a stout cudgel of which he had become possessed, as though determined not to be caught entirely defenseless in case of a sudden raid.

"Do you suppose Jack's really finding out anything?" Buster whispered to Josh when the other leaned down as if to ascertain how the supper was coming on.

"Sure he is," replied the other, "though chances are the cub's giving him taffy just to keep him quiet."

"But Jack seems to be interested a whole lot," objected Buster.

"I think Jack means to join us presently, from the way he nodded to me just then," Josh went on to say hastily, "so don't hurry on the supper more than you can help. For all we know we may have to share it with four instead of one."

It proved to be just as Josh had predicted, for presently Jack left the side of the dark-faced young stranger and come over to the fire.

"Well, how did you manage to get on with him?" asked Josh impetuously.

"It grew easier as we went on," said Jack. "He knows just a little bit of English, after all. When that failed he resorted to the paper and pencil, or else made gestures. When I shook my head to tell him it was all a mystery to me, he would try again in a different way, and we always succeeded in getting there by one means or another."

"Did he own up in the end, Jack?" asked Josh.

"If you mean about being one of the four Serbian youths we thought he might be, he denied it absolutely," came the reply.

"H'm! What else could you expect, since their game had been knocked on the head by the breaking out of the war and they found themselves being hunted like rats in a hostile territory, afraid to ask for anything to eat because they'd like as not be grabbed? No wonder he looks hungry, say I."

Jack looked at the other and shook his head.

"This time you're away off, old fellow," he told Josh. "He didn't come up into Austria-Hungary on an errand of blood, but one of mercy."

"As how, Jack?" asked Buster, already deeply interested.

"He has a little sister," the other went on to say. "She seems to be just so high," and he held his hand about three feet from the ground, "from which I'd judge she might be something like six or seven years old."

"A sister, eh?" George remarked skeptically.

"Listen, fellows," continued Jack, "here's the story he told me as near as I was able to make it out, for lots of times I had to just guess at things; but it ran fairly smooth, after all. He lived in Belgrade, the capital of Serbia. There was his mother, a widow with some means, and one little sister. This girl, it seems, was blind and the pet of everybody who knew her."

"Gee! that sounds interesting," muttered Josh.

"Some time ago the mother learned of a celebrated surgeon up in Budapest who had performed wonderful cures with people afflicted just as the little child was. It was determined to take the girl to him, and an appointment was made; but just then the mother had the misfortune to sprain her ankle and could not walk a step."

"Tough luck," said Buster, "and I can see what the boy did. He looks like he had the grit to carry anything like that out, sure he does."

Apparently Buster was taking stock in Jack's story and changing his opinion again with regard to the dark-faced young stranger.

"Yes, there was nothing for it but that the boy go to Budapest with his little sister and stay there while the operation went on. From what he tells me he was in the Hungarian capital nearly a month. The surgeon operated, and the thing turned out a splendid success. You ought to have seen how his face lighted up when he told me in sign language that she could see now just as well as any one."

"Then why didn't he start home right away, knowing how anxious his mother must be?" asked George incredulously.

"First the surgeon would not allow it for a certain time after the bandages were taken off. Then, as luck would have it, just when they were about to start, a thief broke into their apartment and stole every dollar, or whatever money the Serbians use."

"Oh, how tough that was!" exclaimed Buster sympathetically.

"A likely story, I call it," muttered George.

"On top of it all the war broke out, and he knew that unless they hurried off from Budapest the Hungarian authorities might arrest them. So they sold a few of their things and get enough money together to carry them part of the way to the Serbian border. Then they had to leave the train and start to tramp the rest of the way. Neither of them have had a bite this whole day. Seeing us land, he became desperate and determined to appeal to us to help him, if we looked as if we were kind people. Then I chanced to run across him. That's what he told me, as near as I could make it out."

Jack saw that while Buster and Josh were disposed to believe the young stranger, George still hung back.

"It makes a pretty interesting story, that's right," was what George said, "but there's a fishy part to it. That little sister sounds like an invention to get our sympathy. Where is she at, I'd like to know; let him produce the kid, say I."

CHAPTER XIV

FRIENDS IN TIME OF NEED

"That's so, Jack; unless he can produce the little sister we've got to believe his fine yarn is all a fraud," Josh observed seriously.

"Did you say as much to him, Jack?" questioned George.

"I did," came the ready reply.

"And what was his reply to that?" asked Buster.

"I gathered from his gestures and actions," explained Jack, "that he stood ready, yes, and anxious, to go into the woods near by and get his sister, if only we gave him permission. So I thought I'd put it up to the rest of you first."

"Oh, tell him to go and fetch her along," sneered George. "If he really has got a little sister, and she's hungry, why, I'd be willing to go on half rations myself to help out. I may be suspicious of him, but there isn't a stingy bone in my whole body."

"We know that, George," Jack told him quickly, "and since you seem willing I'll let the poor fellow know about it right away. You can see how eagerly he's watching us now, because he understands what I'm telling you."

"Tell him supper's about ready, and that he ought to hurry," explained Buster.

Jack had another short interview with the young Serbian. Then the other sprang hastily to his feet and ran off, looking back once or twice, and smiling as he waved his hand toward Jack.

"Good-by!" called out George derisively, and then, turning to the others, he added: "Because I hardly expect to see him again, unless he comes back with the other three. Chances are he knew we'd got on to his game, and means to slip away now so he couldn't be nabbed by the authorities."

"Shame on you, George, you old unbeliever!" cried Buster.

"Wait and see who's right," warned the other sturdily, for George always clung to his belief until convinced that he was wrong, when he would frankly confess his error of judgment.

A minute, two of them, passed, and still the boy did not return. It would really seem as though he had had time to go to where he left his sister concealed at the time he crept toward the landing spot of the cruising party in the motorboat, and come back again.

George was grinning with that important air of his, which, being interpreted, meant the usual "I told you so."

Then Josh, whose sharp eyes had detected a moving figure in the semi-gloom, exclaimed:

"There they come over yonder, I do believe!"

"Two or four?" questioned Buster.

"It's all right, boys," Josh continued, for he was standing on a stump, and in this position could see what was invisible to the others.

"Then he's got his little sister along with him, has he?" asked Buster.

"Sure thing," reported Josh, "and as for you, old croaker George, it'd be doing the right thing for you to beg everybody's pardon, and especially the boy's, for thinking such mean things about him."

"Who was the first to guess that he must be one of that band of desperate Serbian youths, tell me?" demanded George. "I was wrong, I'll admit, but an ounce of prevention is always better than a whole pound of cure."

With that he threw away the club which he had been gripping, as though in company with it went all his suspicions.

Presently the Serbian boy came into camp, holding by the hand a pretty dark-eyed little maid of about seven. The boys were immediately smitten with her charms, and no longer wondered that her brother had so openly boasted she was the prettiest little girl in all Belgrade.

Apparently that noted surgeon had done a splendid job, for never had they looked into brighter and more roguish eyes than she possessed. If they had been dulled by cataracts, as Jack suspected was the case, then the curtains had been skillfully removed.

Buster immediately announced that supper was all ready, and would be spoiled by any further waiting; so they sat down, places being prepared for the guests of honor.

While they ate the boys kept up a conversation among themselves. Jack from time to time would hold communication with the Serbian youth, whose appetite proved the truth of his assertion that no food had passed his lips during the whole of the preceding day.

Later on Buster amused himself trying to talk with the little girl and teach her a few words in English. Jack and Josh and George got their heads together, being desirous of settling on what they ought to do with regard to the pair cast adrift in a strange and hostile land.

"They can stay with us all night, anyway, and have breakfast in the morning," suggested Josh.

"And we could make up a little purse among us," added the now penitent George, "enough to carry them across the border and into their own country."

"That's fine of you to mention that, George," Jack told him, "but you are forgetting something. Serbia is at war with Austria, and so you see no trains can be running to the border that would allow a Serbian young fellow to pass. If he ever gets across the river to Belgrade it must be with our help."

"You've got a plan fixed, I guess, Jack?"

"I've been thinking it over, and wanted to hear what your ideas might be before I mentioned it," the other explained. "But, now that you ask me, I'll tell you what I'd like to do. We can find room for them aboard the boat when we start in the morning. Unless we are overhauled on the way there'd be little danger on account of our having Serbians with us, a boy and a child at that."

"I agree with you there, Jack," said George, now evidently seeking to make all amends possible for having allowed himself to believe the stranger a desperate character, when in truth he was only a kind and protecting big brother.

"Ditto here," added Josh glibly, as though he were a parrot.

"We will have to tie up by the time another night comes along," continued Jack, "and if it's cloudy we can hope to try and pass the hostile batteries by keeping in the middle of the river and just floating with the current, never showing a single light. But before that we might make a landing on the Serbian side and put the brother and sister ashore."

Josh and George exchanged looks, nodding their heads as if in approval.

"Now, I call that a good scheme, if you want to know it," declared the former.

"And as Buster is always ready to agree to anything Jack says," George remarked, "I move we call it unanimous."

The readiness of his chums to fall in with his proposition, of course, pleased Jack. He always made it a point to invite the fullest discussion when offering any plan of campaign, because it was better that all of them should feel that they had a hand in engineering matters.

So it was settled, later on Buster being told the arrangements. As George had prophesied, the fat boy had not the slightest objection to make; indeed, he was enthusiastic over the idea of helping the little Serbian girl get back home to her anxious mother.

Arrangements for sleeping were soon effected. As their guests had no blankets, George and Buster insisted on loaning them one each. They said they could go without easily enough; though Jack finally induced George to share his covers, while Josh compelled the fat chum to crawl under with him.

The night passed without anything occurring to disturb them. Everybody slept after a fashion, though doubtless the boys were not as comfortable as though each possessed his own blanket.

It made them feel that they were suffering in a good cause, however, when they saw how happy both the boy and his sister seemed in the morning. The dark clouds that had of late been hanging over their heads had apparently taken flight, and with the rising sun they smiled, and seemed contented with having found such good friends.

After breakfast they started down the river again. It might prove to be the last day of peace for them for some time, since Jack figured that by another sunset they would very likely have reached the scene of hostilities, when danger might be lying in wait for them at every turn.

Of course, all of them were more or less concerned about the prospect of being held up again by some Austrian river war vessel. The presence of Serbians aboard the motorboat would look suspicious in those trying days, and might get the boys into trouble. Nevertheless, not one of them so much as hinted at any desire to be rid of their guests.

The little girl was so winsome that she had captured all their hearts by storm, and they could not do too much for her.

As the afternoon began to pass Jack looked earnestly ahead many times. He wondered what awaited them in that mysterious region whence they were headed. All sorts of strange things might crop up to confront them as they proceeded on their dangerous course; still, no one even gave the idea of turning back a thought.

He had managed to let the Serbian boy know what they meant to do about getting his sister and himself on his native soil. How those black eyes snapped as the plan was unfolded to him! Jack fancied he could see unshed tears there also, showing how their generosity must have affected the other. He could not express his gratitude by repeating that one word "thank" again, but he did display it by almost fiercely seizing Jack's hand and actually kissing it, an act that made the American boy feel exceedingly queer, because he was not accustomed to such things.

They kept, as a rule, closer to the right bank of the river, for that would in time prove to be the one on which the Serbian capital was located. Besides, Jack believed it would answer their purposes better in case circumstances forced them to make a hurried landing, so that their passengers might conceal themselves in the brush.

The sun was hot again, and as the afternoon began to wear along they found that the breeze created by their own swift passage was the only invigorating thing to be met with.

"But it's beginning to cloud up, you can see," Josh remarked, when Buster complained that he was melting away with the heat; "and once the old sun gets out of sight it'll be a whole lot more comfy."

"I've been watching those clouds," remarked Jack, "and they please me a whole lot, because we must have a cloudy night if we're ever going to run past the batteries on both sides of the river."

"Whew! that sounds as if we might be away back in the civil war, trying to pass Memphis on a gunboat, with the Confeds whanging away at us to beat the band. But, of course, you don't expect to have any real trouble getting by, do you, Jack?"

"So far as I can see, there's no reason why we should meet up with any," the skipper informed him.

"And once we're well by Belgrade the worst will be over," cheerily observed Josh. "You see, the railroad runs down through Serbia from the capital, and any invasion must, of course, follow the Morava River, because Serbia is a mountainous country, and there are passes through which troops have to go if ever they hope to reach Nisch down near the middle of the nation."

"Seems like you've been reading up on Serbia, Josh," ventured George.

"I have, all about the last war between the Balkan States," Josh admitted. "And let me tell you right here, if the Austrians and the Germans ever try to invade that little country of born fighters they'll find they've bitten off more than they can chew. The Serbians know every foot of ground, and can lay in ambush on the heights, dropping rocks down on the enemy, and using all sorts of quick-firing guns to cut them down in windrows."

"If only all these Balkan countries were agreed on a single policy," said Jack, "they could snap their fingers at the Teuton alliance, for no force could ever be brought to bear against them that would smash their defenses. But petty jealousies keep them apart, and may be their undoing in the end."

The sun vanished about this time, the clouds having risen far enough to cover his blazing face.

"That feels a heap better," announced the panting Buster; "and it looks like we mightn't glimpse old Sol again to-day. For one I'm glad. Sunshine is all very well in winter time, but when it's hot summer I prefer the shade."

The others laughed at his odd way of putting it, for Buster often expressed himself in a peculiar fashion. Josh said he "mixed his metaphors," though Buster was never able to get him to explain what he meant by saying that.

Just then something came stealing to their ears that caused the boys to exchange meaning glances. It was a distant grumbling that died away almost as soon as it reached them, a sort of complaining, reverberating boom that brought a thrill with it.

CHAPTER XV

THE BOOMING OF BIG GUNS

"Another storm coming, worse luck!" grumbled George.

"Going to spoil all our fine plans in the bargain," added Josh; "for if it turns out to be anything as bad as that other whooper, excuse me from wanting to be out on the river in the middle of the night."

"Listen again!" said Jack, with a meaning in his manner.

"There she goes, and I must say it's kind of queer thunder, after all," Buster advanced; "each growl is separate and distinct, and not like anything I ever heard before."

"Sure enough," continued Josh; and then, as though a sudden light had dawned upon him, he turned to Jack to add: "Say, you don't imagine now, do you, that can be the booming of big guns we are listening to?"

Jack nodded his head in the affirmative.

"It must be," he said positively.

"Sounds just like blasts," continued Josh, "up in the quarry near our town, when they let the same off by electricity at noon, when the men are all out of the workings. Boom! boom! boom! boom! Let me tell you they must be making things hum over there now, with all that firing going on."

"What do you suppose they're doing, Jack?" asked George.

"For one thing sending shells into Belgrade," came the reply.

"Look, the Serbian boy has caught on as well as the rest of us," said Josh, "and it frets him a whole lot, too, you can see by his face. Now he's talking with the little sister, and pointing, as if he might be explaining what that sound means."

"Well, can you blame him for feeling that way?" burst out Buster; "when you must remember that their mother is somewhere in Belgrade, and with those shells bursting in the city they may get home only to find that they have been left orphans. I guess war is all that General Sherman said it was."

"Oh, shucks! We haven't seen hardly anything of its horrors yet. Wait till you read what is happening in Belgium about this time, and then it'll be time to talk," George told him.

"But why didn't we hear the cannonading before?" asked Buster; "it seemed to hit us all of a sudden."

"Because there was a shift of the wind," explained Jack. "You know it was on our right before, and since then has changed, so that now it seems to be coming straight from the south."

As they kept on down the river the sounds, reaching their ears every once in so often, increased gradually in volume.

Every time the suggestive sound came to their ears it could be seen that the two young Serbians would start and listen eagerly. Undoubtedly their thoughts must be centered on the home they had left in Belgrade, and they were wondering if the latest shell could have dropped anywhere near that dearly loved spot.

"Honest, now," said Josh presently, "after that last shot I could hear a second fainter crash, which I take it may have been the shell exploding in or over the city."

"It may have been a Serbian gun, after all," George asserted, "and if so, then the shoe was on the other foot, and the shell burst in the fortifications on the Austrian side of the Danube, perhaps scattering guns and soldiers around as if they were so many logs."

"That's what our friend here is hoping deep down in his heart, you can be sure," Jack mentioned, with a glance toward the boy passenger.

"Look away down yonder and tell me if that isn't one of those monitors like my cousin Captain Stanislaus commands," said George just then.

Josh tested his eagle eye and admitted that, while the surface of the river was misty, which fact made seeing difficult, he believed the other was right, and that the object they were looking at did resemble a "cheese-box on a raft" in marine architecture.

"Then we can't be so very far above Belgrade," Jack concluded.

"You mean the monitor may have been doing some of that shelling, do you?" questioned Buster.

"I don't know about that, for none of us have seen any sign of firing aboard the boat; but she's evidently anchored there to take part in protecting the Austrian troops that will soon be attempting to cross to hostile territory. So we must expect to haul in somewhere along here and wait for night to settle down."

"It would be too risky to try and pass the monitor, I reckon you mean?" George asked.

"You remember how we were brought up with a round turn the other time," he was reminded; "and if we refused to obey the summons to come alongside a second shot would sink us like a stone."

"Whee! if one of those big shells ever struck this chip of a boat there wouldn't be enough of her left for firewood," asserted Josh. "So I say just as you do, Jack; we mustn't be too brash and take chances. We can't expect to fight the whole Austrian navy on the Danube. The word for us is diplomacy, remember that. We've got to play the Napoleon style of strategy if we hope to win out in this game."

Jack allowed the boat to continue on her course for some little time longer. He did not mean to take unnecessary chances, but at the same time the further they were down the river before night set in the better, since it would shorten the time they expected to be in the danger zone.

He kept a wary eye on the anchored monitor, for all of them could by this time plainly see that it was one of those strange looking vessels, believed by Austria to be just suited to the waters of the Danube for offense and defense.

When not employed in this fashion Jack was watching the near-by shore for a favorable landing spot. They could proceed to make a fire and act as though fully intending to spend the night there. If by accident they had visitors from the monitor early in the evening they could arrange it so that nothing suspicious would be seen.

The firing had now ceased for the time being, as though enough had been accomplished on either side for the day.

It was not long before they found themselves up against the bank. Jack had picked out a good landing place, for there were trees in plenty, under which they could make themselves comfortable.

"Do you think they have noticed us across there on board the monitor?" Buster asked, as they stepped ashore.

"It would be strange if they hadn't," Josh told him. "Of course, they can see all that goes on up and down the river, and we were in plain sight. Jack, did you expect they might have a pair of field glasses leveled on us, and was that why you had the brother and sister keep inside the cabin lately?"

"Well," replied the skipper, "I saw something flash over there while the sun was shining through that rift in the clouds, and I got the idea they might be using their binoculars. You see, if they should send over to interview us, and the two Serbians were absent from the camp, as we mean they shall be, what could we say if asked about them? That was why I wanted them to keep out of sight, while the four of us remained in full view."

Josh did not say anything further, but the look of admiration he gave Jack told what his thoughts were. In his mind the other could not be equalled when it came to covering the whole ground and laying out extensive plans, for Jack seemed to be able to grasp everything.

"We must keep a watch out on the river and try to be on our guard," continued the leader. "If they send a boat over here to investigate, we ought to know about it before the men have a chance to land and spy on our camp."

The boat was tied up, and Buster had already taken ashore all he needed for the evening meal; while Josh was making a fire in the midst of some stones he had collected in a sort of cairn.

The day had ended in a dismal fashion for one starting out so bravely with blue skies and plenty of warm sunshine. Out over the water the haze was thickening, so that when George gave place to Josh later on it was next door to impossible to tell where the Austrian monitor was anchored.

"I've lined it up with this stone here and that tree out on the little point," George explained; "the boat lies almost directly with the two, so if you happen to see any light over there you'll know what it means, Josh," he told the other, as he gave up his post.

"As long as you could see the monitor, were there any signs of a boat leaving?" he asked; but George shook his head and told him he had seen nothing suspicious.

CHAPTER XVI

UNDER COVER OF NIGHT

Some time later, when George again relieved Josh at the outlook post, the latter came strolling up to the little fire to get his supper, of which he was in need, for Josh had a pretty healthy appetite that seldom went back on him.

"One thing sure," he remarked, as he sat himself down and prepared to have Buster wait on him, "when you told me, Jack, to build this fire so it couldn't be easily seen from out on the river, you knew what you were talking about."

"Well," remarked the commodore simply, "my idea at the time was to avoid having the light noticed too easily by any one who happened to be on the water. Yes, and I hoped to keep the people on that monitor a mile and more away from wanting to pay us a visit too early in the night."

"It might break up our plans all right if they did come," agreed Josh, lifting his tincup to his lips and proceeding to let some of the fine coffee pass down his throat as a "bracer" or opening of ceremonies.

"As long as you stayed out there at the point, did you see or hear anything suspicious, Josh?" Buster wanted to know, when he handed the platter, heaped up with good things, to the late-comer.

"Never a sign all the time I stood sentry," came the reply, though Josh had a little difficulty in talking and eating at the same time. "But please let me take the edge off my ferocious appetite before you throw any more questions at me, fellows. I'll be in a more angelic humor then, mebbe."

"Angelic—that's pretty rich for you, Josh," gurgled Buster; but, having enough sympathy for a hungry chum to know how Josh felt, he maintained a discreet silence after that.

Jack walked over to the near-by shore. He wanted to find out for himself how matters seemed to be going.

"Hello! That you, Jack?" said a voice suddenly, when he found himself close to the brim of the river.

It had become so dark by this time, the moon not having as yet arisen behind the clouds, that seeing was next to impossible. George, however, had heard footsteps somewhere close by, and guessed who was coming.

"Yes, where are you, George? Oh, I see you, now that you move. That's the boat just beyond you, too. Everything lovely with you?"

"I heard something across the river that sounded as if it might be a boat being lowered that struck against the side of the monitor. Then there were voices, too. You know how queer sounds come across a mile or more of water, Jack?"

"Yes, of course I do. But if it was a boat being lowered we'll have to change our plans somewhat," Jack continued.

"By that you mean get away from here sooner?" queried the vidette.

"Just what I do, George."

"Suppose now it was a boat being put in the water that I heard, though I may have been mistaken; how long would it take them to row over here, do you think?" George asked next.

"That depends on how hard they handled the oars," said Jack. "It could hardly be less than half an hour at the best, I should say. You see, the monitor lies down-stream from here, so they'd have to first of all work against the strong current before crossing."

"Yes, and then again it might be they'd try to keep us from hearing them coming all they could, Jack, which would mean they couldn't put all their strength into the work."

"You've got the right idea, George; so we can have something like half an hour to get away in. It may turn out to be a false alarm after all, but we can't afford to take any chances."

"That's so," agreed the other briskly, for a wonder, never dreaming of offering any objection. "The sooner we're abroad on the river the better. Then again, before the old moon comes up behind the clouds, we'll have it pitch dark. That ought to help us a lot about slipping past without getting caught."

"Stay here, and keep on listening, George."

"Are you going back to get the rest of the crowd, Jack?"

"Yes. As soon as Josh has finished his supper we had better go aboard again and shove off," he was informed.

"But say, tell me how you expect to work it, please Jack, before you go."

"If you mean the boat, that's a simple thing," the skipper told him. "You know we've got a strong push-pole that's a pretty good length? Well, I took soundings as we came in toward the shore, and found that the river is fairly shallow around here. With that pole we can push out into the stream quite a little distance. Then we'll just lie low and let her float on the current."

"Well, now, I sort of expected that would be the programme," said George; "and I certainly agree with you there. Silence is our best asset in a game like this. We'd feel pretty cheap and small after getting well started if all of a sudden some one called out of the darkness: 'Tag—you're it!'"

George, finding Jack had slipped away meanwhile, and that he was merely talking to empty space, drew the line at wasting his breath in this manner, and relapsed into silence.

When Jack got back to the little fire he found that, short though the time had been, Josh had made rapid headway with his supper. The pannikin was already more than half empty, and that must be his third cup of coffee Buster was pouring out for him.

Everybody looked up as Jack came into camp.

"You'll have just five minutes more, Josh, to finish your supper," was the first thing the other said as he joined them.

Josh looked surprised.

"What! so soon?" he exclaimed, and then started in to devour his food ravenously, as though determined to make the best of the limited time.

Buster laughed softly.

"Josh, you make me think of that old, old fellow who had his gravestone cut, and kept it in the house for about thirty years. The neighbors were wild with curiosity to know what he had put on the same, leaving a blank for the date of his departure. After he was buried every one flocked to the cemetery to read it. And this was what they found chiseled in the stone: 'I expected this—but not so soon!'"

Josh did not make any reply. He was indeed too busy to even laugh just then, for in his mind the seconds were trooping past, and it went against his grain to waste good food.

When three minutes had passed he was ready. Meanwhile Jack had glanced around to make sure they left nothing behind them in the shape of a blanket or cooking utensil, none of which he felt they could spare.

"There, I'm all ready for business!" announced Josh, climbing to his feet, for he was really too full of supper to move with his accustomed agility.

"Everybody get hold of something, then," said Jack, "and we'll head for the boat. I'll scatter the fire last of all. That's the true hunter way, you know, never to leave a fire burning behind, because a wind may come up and scatter the red ashes among the dead leaves. Many a forest fire has sprung from just that folly. But in our case we've got another reason for wanting to kill the blaze; it may keep some people guessing to know what's become of us."

Presently all this had been accomplished, and they were heading, Indian file, toward the river bank. Josh led the way, laden down with things. Then came the Serbian boy, and his little sister, who clung to him through it all; after them Buster stumbled with his customary awkwardness, while Jack brought up the rear to make sure that no one strayed from the line.

They soon arrived at the edge of the bank, where George joined them. Buster, as he looked anxiously out at the bank of gloom marking the river, felt a strange sensation taking possession of him. It was not fear, though possibly the feeling could be likened to awe.

"Makes me think of the smugglers landing on the coast of England, and trying to evade the revenue officers with their casks of spirits," he whispered to Josh.

Somehow, although as yet Jack had said nothing on that score, even Buster seemed to realize that there was great need for caution, which was why he lowered his voice in the way he did.

The next thing was to get aboard the boat. Jack saw to it first of all that the brother and sister were safe, and then urged Buster to follow suit.

"Josh, I'm going to appoint you to the honor task," he went on to say softly.

"Good for you, Jack," came the low reply; "just tell me what I'm to do?"

"George will go aboard with me, for we want to get the push-pole handy. When I give a whistle, unfasten the cable and shove her off, climbing over the side yourself the best way you can. Get that, Josh?"

"Just my style, boss," he heard the other say as he started toward the tree to which the strong rope was attached.

Jack had examined his chart many times lately, so that he knew just where they must be on the river. The Danube takes a sharp turn toward the east at Belgrade, and here the Save River empties into the larger stream. On the same shore that the little party had chosen for their landing lies the Austrian town of Semlin; and here on the heights strong fortifications have long menaced the Serbian capital, as well as other batteries further along the Danube.

It would be impossible for them to land above Belgrade in order to let their passengers go ashore, so on this account it was necessary that they take the two with them while running the batteries.

Jack had regretted this, because he did not like the idea of that innocent child sharing their danger; still, so far as he could see, there was nothing else to be done. The Serb begged him not to think of abandoning them while on hostile territory. He had explained by gestures and pictures that his father had been a general in the Serbian army, and on account of the hatred borne for his family by the Hungarians he felt sure something terrible would happen if they fell into the hands of the enemy and their identity were discovered.

When Jack had everything in readiness for their hasty departure he gave the low whistle for which Josh on shore was impatiently waiting. They could hear him pulling the cable from around the tree trunk; then it came aboard, and Josh started pushing the boat off.

This required no great effort, for the water was sufficient to float such a small craft comfortably. Having managed to get the boat started, Josh clambered aboard and, being a nimble fellow, even though far from himself after that hearty supper, he contrived to accomplish this without any particular noise.

"We're off!" said George softly, but with considerable satisfaction, as he felt the motorboat moving under the impetus Jack was giving to the push-pole.

"Bully!" echoed Buster, though at the time he probably hardly knew whether he could call himself satisfied or not; for he realized that they were taking more or less desperate chances in trying to slip down the river when two hostile armies were spread along the opposite banks watching for any sign of a surprise and doubtless ready to start a hot fire at the first indication of a crossing being attempted.

This was especially true of the Serbians, for they knew that an invasion of their territory was planned by the Austrian army, backed by heavy artillery.

Jack continued to handle that pole with more or less ability. It was no new task for him. Any one who goes much upon the water in motorboats learns the value of a good pole, especially when the cruise leads through swampy sections, where it is no uncommon thing to be mired and need other help than that afforded by the unreliable engine.

The current began to make itself felt almost immediately they were off. It was Jack's intention to keep on using his pole until he could no longer touch bottom. When that time arrived they would have to let the boat drift with the current, under the belief that it was apt to stay fairly well out in the river.

"Listen, everybody," said Jack about this time; "from now on silence is going to be the golden rule aboard this craft. Don't say a single word unless you have to, and then whisper it. That applies to every one."

The night was fairly quiet about this time, at least there was no firing from the batteries on the banks of the Danube, though thousands upon thousands of armed men kept watch there, ready to lock arms in a fierce battle when the time came.

Long had this feeling of bitter enmity lain deep down in the hearts of Austrian and Serb. The dual monarchy had for many years looked upon the smaller kingdom as a tempting morsel that some day she hoped to engulf into her capacious maw, just as had been done in the case of Bosnia and other countries now forming parts of the Austrian patchwork of many tongues and many people, all under the rule of Francis Joseph. And now at last war had actually broken out, so that the scores of many years would all have a chance of being settled before peace came again to distracted Europe.

Deeper grew the water, so that Jack was beginning to find some difficulty in reaching bottom. This meant that presently there would be no further need of the push-pole, for they would have gotten out far enough to let the stream carry them along.

It was about this time that sounds came stealing over the water, causing fresh alarm. All of them could make out the distinct creak of oars in rowlocks, being worked with a steady rhythm that told of experienced hands in the unseen boat.

Then the next thing they heard was a low muttered word of command, which came from exactly the same quarter as the other noise.

A boat was passing toward the shore they had recently left. It must have come from over the river, and, as the monitor lay in that quarter, evidently those who had been sent out to investigate the status of the motorboat party had seen fit to pull straight across first, intending to follow the trend of the shore up to the camp.

Jack had reason to believe they would pass down before the hostile boat drew close enough for any one to make them out; nevertheless, his heart seemed to cease beating for the moment, such was the intense anxiety that seized upon him.

CHAPTER XVII

AMIDST BURSTING SHELLS

Jack did not even dare attempt to draw the push-pole up out of the water, lest he manage in some fashion to strike it against the side of the boat, and in this way draw the attention of the enemy.

Everything depended on luck—and the current of the river. If this latter proved strong enough to draw the motorboat far enough away, so that its outlines could not be distinguished by those in the rowboat, all might yet be well. Certainly if hearty wishes could accomplish anything this end was likely to be achieved, for every one aboard was hoping it would come to pass.

Jack soon began to breathe easier. He felt sure the boat would pass back of them, and at a sufficient distance to avoid discovery, unless something unexpected came about to betray their presence. A sneeze just then would have ruined everything; and Buster felt a cold chill pass over him when he had such an inclination. He managed to ward the desire off by rubbing both sides of his nose violently, just as he had been taught to do by his mother when in church.

So the sounds died out, and they now heard nothing save the gurgle of the water or the sighing of the summer breeze among the treetops on shore.

Far away across the river he caught sight of a light. It was low down and close to the water, so Jack could easily guess it marked the spot where the Austrian monitor lay anchored.

Upon making another trial with the pole Jack found it possible to still touch bottom. As it was his desire to keep on pressing out as far as they could go, so as to approach near the middle of the river, he continued to exert himself. Every yard gained counted for just so much, and now was the time to do it. Later on the opportunity would have passed, and it might be too late.

When they arrived at the point where the Save joined forces with the Danube it was expected that the influence of this new flow of water would add to the swiftness of their passage.

Jack knew that it would be an hour of greatest anxiety while they remained in the region dominated by those big guns. At any minute they might be discovered by some unlucky accident, such as the moon coming out from her concealment, or the breeze rising so as to carry away the gathering fog.

He had everything ready so that the engine could be started up instantly should they have reason to believe they were seen from the Austrian shore. As a last resort he was intending to make for the Serbian bank, in hopes of finding shelter there. At least, if captured by the Serbs, they would be treated decently, once the identity of their passengers had been learned.

The minutes crept slowly past.

All they could do was to sit there and turn their heads to look eagerly first this way and then that.

Feeling a tug at his sleeve, Jack turned toward Josh, who was closest to him.

"Look yonder; there are lights, Jack!" whispered the other in his ear.

Jack guessed that this must be Belgrade, though at the time the Serbian capital, being the subject of bombardment, lay almost in darkness, so that the vigilant foe across the river might not have the range.

Somehow it interested Jack deeply to see those few meager lights where at other times the sky might have blazed with the electric glow, for Belgrade was always a little Paris of the Balkans. It seemed to speak of the terrible results that must follow in the train of a brutal war, civilization giving way to barbarity.

And there off to the right must be the Save River, flowing from far up in the region between the Croatian and the Bosnian provinces of Austria.

Back of this stream he knew there were heavy fortifications dominating the distant Serbian capital. It would seem that Austria had taken particular pains to threaten her fiery little neighbor on the south, possibly in hopes of some day stirring up another hornets' nest in the Balkans, through which she might attain her selfish ends and annex new territory.

As their course did not lie in that direction Jack bothered himself not at all in connection with the Save batteries. He was, however, deeply interested in the ones he knew were located upon the lower heights. What peril they must face would spring from this source.

It was perhaps only natural that just then Jack should suddenly remember what had been said about searchlights. He wondered whether any were in use in this section of the fighting zone. Germans, French and British would certainly have carried such necessary appliances with them, but it was uncertain whether the Serbs or the Austrians had seen fit to install them here.

Now they seemed to be sweeping around the bend in the river. Jack could feel a new motion to the boat, which he believed must come from the addition of the Save waters to those of the Danube.

He watched both shores alternately. It was almost impossible to make out anything except where some height was dimly outlined against the clouded sky line. Then he turned his eyes aloft. The moon had risen, for in the east it was light compared to the west, though nothing of her silvery disc could be discovered.

Would the clouds continue to befriend the fugitives of the Danube through the dangerous passage of the batteries? If there came a break above even for a brief interval it might spell ruin for their hopes. And so Jack hoped most fervently that the clouds would prove merciful and keep on shutting off that light which, coming at an unfortunate moment, might mean their betrayal.

Without the slightest warning there came a sudden fearful sound. At the same instant they saw a vivid flash far back on the Austrian heights. Seconds followed, marked by the accelerated pulsations of their hearts. Then followed a crash and a flash over the place where the boys knew the capital lay in darkness and gloom.

The bombardment of Belgrade had begun again. Some plan of campaign was being followed out that had to do with either the utter destruction of the city or else the rout of its defenders, so that a hostile army could make the crossing in safety, something they did not dare attempt as long as the Serbs remained in their trenches awaiting their coming.

The mere fact of its being night made no difference. Long ago the Austrians had undoubtedly platted everything out and secured the range for their big guns on the heights back of the river. They could fire just as accurately in utter darkness as in broad daylight, for the shells were hurled with mathematical precision, each one being timed to explode at a certain second.

As if that first shot were looked upon as a defiance, several Serb guns took up the challenge. It was inspiring to see the shells burst like giant skyrockets far up on the heights. Evidently others besides the Austrians had occupied their spare time in getting distances all down to a fine point, for the Serbian gunners managed to drop their projectiles in given places, where they threatened to smash some of the tremendous war engines of the enemy.

The boys knew that it was much too late for them to think of turning back now. In fact, such a thing was utterly impossible, much as they might have wished it. All they could do was to keep on floating down the river, trusting in their customary good luck to escape harm.

They could hear strange noises as the reverberations died out, which Jack knew must be made by the whizzing shells far above them. It gave him a thrill to realize the fact that he and his three chums were thus brought into the very whirlwind of war, with deadly engines of destruction busy on all sides of them.

Even the anchored monitor several miles up the river joined in the music, for that partly muffled roar seemed to come from the direction they knew her to be in.

The two passengers had remained perfectly silent all this while, though their faces kept turned toward the spot where they knew the darkened city must lie. It was easy for Jack to imagine what their thoughts must be at such a time as this. No one could say how long this bombardment had been going on, or what sort of damage the terrible shells exploding may have done among the numerous fine buildings of the Serbian capital.

By now it might be lying a mass of ruins for aught they knew; and somewhere in the midst their mother had been living the last they heard from her. Yes, Jack could easily appreciate what agonies of mind the couple must be enduring as they crouched there in each other's arms, and with throbbing hearts listened to the hoarse crash of the opposing guns, the one friendly and the other freighted with hatred and animosity.

There was, of course, no danger to the party on the motorboat from the shells that were passing so high overhead, describing a parabola in their flight, something after the manner of a rainbow. Jack's fears were along other lines.

If, as he suspected, this night bombardment on the part of the Austrian batteries was meant to occupy the attention of their foes while a force of troops was being ferried over the river or a temporary bridge made of pontoons and planks thrown across, it would mean that sooner or later the fugitives must be brought up with a round turn and find themselves caught in a trap.

One shell burst prematurely, and almost overhead, giving them a severe shock, for the sound was deafening. All of them involuntarily dropped down and held their breath in suspense. Then they heard missiles striking the water all around with an angry hiss, some of them terribly close.

"Nothing doing!" muttered Josh, when the fusillade had stopped and it became evident that they had escaped being struck.

"It was a narrow escape, all the same," said Jack, with deep gratitude in his voice, though at the same time he remembered to keep his tones low.

All of them were fervently hoping there would be no more short fuses with the shells that were screaming overhead. It was bad enough to be passing underneath such a rain of fire without incurring the added peril of being unintentionally struck.

Back and forth the duel continued. The Serbian gunners were evidently bent on giving as good as they received. They also hoped, no doubt, to make things so warm up there on the heights that the Austrians would cease firing in order to save their guns from being dismounted.

Every yard counted for the fugitives. Hope grew stronger in the heart of Buster as they continued to glide along on the bosom of the river and nothing happened to disturb this feeling of increasing confidence. He really began to believe, perhaps for the first time, that they were going, after all, to float beyond the dangerous zone and find safety below.

As he afterwards declared, Buster lived years during that period of suspense. It seemed to him that minutes must be hours, for each one was fraught with such unlimited possibilities of evil that such things as seconds were not to be reckoned with at all.

The friendly clouds still held the moon from coming forth to betray them, and it was undoubtedly true that they were passing the worst of the line of bombardment. Given just a certain amount of time and they could count themselves safe from that source of danger.

There remained the possibility of coming upon the Austrian forces below starting to bridge the river or cross on boats.

Jack believed that it was not wise for a white man to shout until he was fully out of the woods. While the prospect certainly looked hopeful, he would not allow himself to believe the danger was over until many more miles had been passed.

Between Belgrade and the Iron Gate, which latter is situated at the junction of Austria, Serbia and Rumania, there is a stretch of river nearly a hundred miles in extent. Here the Danube makes another sharp turn amidst wonderful scenery, and for a long distance forms the boundary between Serbia and Rumania.

Jack realized full well that they could not count themselves free from peril until they saw the shore of Rumania on their left. He hardly knew whether it would be wise for them to try and make progress during daylight, for they might be picked up at any time by Austrian soldiers afloat on the river, or made the target of concealed guns ashore, under the impression that the motorboat must belong to Serbs.

Josh, being an ardent chap and easily influenced by outer appearances, actually believed everything was going the right way, and that they had escaped from the jaws of another dilemma. Only for Jack's caution he would very likely have been inclined to voice his delight in some boisterous way; but he did not dare give his feelings full sway.

So far the current had done all they could have asked. It had swept the boat onward persistently, and without any sound to betray them. Before now, doubtless, those men from the anchored monitor must have found where they had built their little cooking fire and learned that the mysterious motorboat had vanished, either down the river or back again whence it came. Jack was not bothering himself in the least about the things that were gone. The wheel of the mill would never turn again with the water that was past, according to his notion.

He kept looking ahead all the time. Something was bothering him, undoubtedly, for Josh discovered that the skipper had his hand up to his ear, as though trying to add to his powers of hearing.

"What is it, Jack?" he whispered.

"I saw lights below, moving lights, and something is going on, I'm afraid," Jack told him. "The sound of the guns deadens everything. I believe it is being kept up on purpose to hide something else. See, you can catch the lights I spoke about now."

"Say, I thought I caught something like hammering just then, Jack," said the other in fresh excitement. "Do you think the Austrians can be trying to get some of their troops across the river under cover of the darkness and fog?"

"I've been afraid we'd find that was the meaning of all the firing," Jack answered. "The Austrians don't dare try it in broad daylight, but hope to push enough men over to-night to hold a bridge-head, and then follow with their field artillery."

"But what would they try to do, cross on boats, Jack?"

"If that was hammering we really heard," came the reply, "then it means they are trying to spread a pontoon bridge across the Danube. Long before dawn they could land thousands of men with many guns on the Serbian side of the river."

CHAPTER XVIII

THE SMASHING OF THE PONTOON BRIDGE

"It must be a bridge they're building," said Josh presently, "because just then I saw a light move along, as if held by some one who was running."

Sounds began to reach them at the same time, which were very significant. On the whole Jack realized that there could no longer be the slightest doubt about the fact that the Austrians were pushing out a pontoon bridge with all the haste they could throw into the undertaking.

Already they seemed to be much more than half-way across the river, having, no doubt, selected a place where it was not unusually wide. And what were the Serbs doing all this while? Had they been caught napping, so that when the dawn broke the enemy would have secured a firm footing on the southern bank of the disputed river and could move the balance of his forces across at his leisure?

It looked that way, though Jack doubted it very much. From what he had read and heard of the people of the smaller kingdom he believed they were too smart not to see through the device of the enemy. He rather fancied they were in force somewhere in the darkness shrouding the southern bank, and that just when the Austrians were congratulating themselves on having met with splendid success something was scheduled to happen calculated to give the invaders a surprise.

Jack realized that it was folly for them to continue down the river. If the pontoon bridge had already reached a point three-quarters of the way across, the workers on it would quickly discover the oncoming motorboat. Indeed, the chances were the craft must bump up against one of the pontoons and could get no further.

This would be bad enough, but Jack fancied there was something ten times more dreadful awaiting them if they reached the swaying structure. Should the waiting Serbs conclude the time had come to put an end to this bridge building, a hurricane of shot and shell would be hurled across the scanty water separating them from the shore, and few there would be who could escape the rain of missiles.

That was no place for neutrals, Jack decided. The only thing that remained for them to do was to make speedily for the shore. To accomplish this desired end it would be necessary for them to start up the engine at once, though Jack meant to keep the muffler in place and cut out all the noise he could, not wishing to draw attention to that quarter.

That was where the benefit of preparedness came in handy. It took him but three seconds to accomplish what he wanted to do. Following the cranking there came a series of explosions that were not very loud, and immediately the boat started off at a lively clip.

Every one waited with more or less nervousness to see if anything happened, but not a shot was fired. Those at work on the swinging bridge were in too feverish a condition of making haste to bother about a few spluttering sounds like that; while the concealed Serbs, if there were really any such near by, did not want to disclose the fact of their presence in the vicinity by doing anything prematurely.

Jack immediately swung the boat around and headed up-stream again. He fancied they were a little too close to the pontoon bridge-builders for safety if anything did happen, as he fully expected would be the case.

When he had gone a short distance he headed for the southern shore, meaning to come to the land and stay there until something was decided, one way or the other.

"Slow up, Jack!" exclaimed Josh, who was shading his eyes with his hand, though more from habit than because he thought it aided him in seeing. "We're close to the bank now."

Cutting off the power, Jack allowed the boat to glide forward. George had taken up the push-pole, and with this he proceeded to help things along. So they presently came into shallow water and ran aground close to the shore, which stood out above them against the gray sky, there being something of a small bluff.

So far everything had worked well. Jack felt they had reason to be more than satisfied with the progress made. Here they could remain in secret and await coming events. If the bridge were finished, and the Austrians commenced passing over, the boys would have to make some new plans looking to the future. Everything depended on the next half hour.

The furious hammering up on the distant heights across the river still continued, and Serbian guns answered every shot, so that it might not appear they were either lacking in ammunition or courage.

There was a stir in the middle of the boat. Jack could easily guess that the two passengers were aware of the fact that they could easily spring over the side and find their feet pressing their native soil. Now was the time for them to go ashore. They could either flee to the interior or else risk everything in entering the capital after the bombardment had ceased once more, in search of the mother, who had been last heard from there.

The boy gripped each one of them by the hand. What he said they could not understand, though it was easy to guess the meaning of his warm words of thanks. They had each one of them to kiss the little girl, for Josh boldly started it and no one wished to be left out.

After that the Serbian lad jumped over the side, standing in water up to his ankles, and lifted his sister to dry ground. The four motorboat chums saw them no more, but they would always remember the incident with pleasure.

After the two had gone Jack breathed more easily. He felt that he could face the future, no matter what it had in store for them, with a better spirit, now that the pretty little girl had been removed from danger in their company. Besides, it must always be a source of satisfaction to himself and mates to remember that they had been enabled to prove of more or less assistance to those who were in deep trouble, with no way out of the difficulty save by the help of the American lads.

"I wonder now if the Serbs are asleep at the switch while all this thing is going on below here?" George said, after a little more time had passed, and they could hear the working human beavers on the pontoon bridge more plainly than ever.

"Don't you believe it," Josh told him. "Look up and see what a splendid ambush this little bluff would make. Well, take my word for it, down below there Serbs are crouching in bunches, waiting with their machine guns until just when it seems the bridge is going to be joined with the shore. Then you'll hear something drop!"

"My stars!" muttered Buster, "I wouldn't want to be one of those poor fellows at work with those pontoons, not for all the gold in King Solomon's mine I wouldn't. They won't have a ghost of a show, I'm afraid."

"But we're far enough away from the place not to be in danger—how about that, Jack?" George went on to say in a cautious tone.

"Only a random shot could come this way, if the Austrians on the other shore start things going. I don't believe they will, because they'll be afraid of hitting their own men."

"This is exciting, all right," ventured Josh.

"Well, better all keep still again," Jack remarked; "we might attract some attention, you know, and that's the last thing we want to do right now. If the bridge is destroyed we can wait a while until things cool off, and then try our luck again, dropping down with the current."

They kept as well behind the side of the boat as possible, acting on Jack's advice, though the thin shell could hardly serve as a means of protection in case a projectile of any sort came that way.

Once more the minutes dragged fearfully, though their suspense was hardly of the same personal nature as before. It seemed to Buster that there was a mine to be exploded out there on the river, and that those soldiers who were working feverishly to complete the bridge must be directly over it. Any second now they might expect to hear a dreadful crash, and catch the shouts of those who were in range of the firing, as well as the rending of the boats under the rain of missiles.

Nearer still the Austrian bridge builders were coming. They had been well trained in their business, those army engineers, and worked methodically, even while laboring under a tremendous strain both of body and mind.

Jack, chancing to come in contact with Buster, found the other shivering as if he had the ague. He knew that it was due to agitation consequent upon excitement. Doubtless the beads of perspiration were rolling down Buster's cheeks at the same time, even though the night air was rather chilly now instead of being warm.

Jack was glad he had been wise enough to come back up the river some little distance before reaching land. If the Austrian batteries turned some of their guns on that shore later, the boys would stand less chance of being hit when the mighty shells exploded along the bluff.

"Oh! I wish it was all over with!" groaned Josh, upon whom the dreadful suspense was telling terribly.

Hardly had he said this than the very atmosphere about them seemed to be rent with a tremendous explosion. A gun had been fired not far away, for the fire blazed forth from the little bluff almost over their heads. There was heard a dreadful rending of planks and boats, accompanied by shouts and shrieks.

This was the opening gun.

Almost immediately there leaped from the shore below the boys what looked like a long zigzag line of fire. Accompanying it came the discordant grinding of numerous machine guns, sending a constant stream of missiles out there upon the swaying pontoon bridge.

The darkness was for the time being dispelled, and the boys saw with staring eyes such a vivid picture as comes seldom in the lives of any one not a soldier. It fascinated even while appalling them by its horrible reality.

The constant flashing of the rapid-fire guns dazzled their eyes, but at the same time they could see the strange low bridge built upon the aligned pontoons. It had been hastily but fairly well constructed, considering that the workmen had to handle their tools in almost utter darkness. Instinct and long practice had to take the place of eyesight.

They were swarming like bees all over the structure even then, some carrying planks and others hurrying back for new burdens. Just on the down-river side the boys could catch glimpses of many who seemed to be pushing other pontoons out, by holding on to the part of the bridge already finished. These they expected to use in filling the remaining gap between the present terminus of the bridge and the intended anchorage on the bank.

Alas! they were never given the opportunity to carry out their well-laid plans. That hurricane of lead and iron was sweeping everything before it. Men were going down by dozens; some plunged from the bridge into the river, seeking to take the chances of being drowned to the certainty of death in that hailstorm of deadly messengers.

Every conceivable manner of outcry could be heard. Men shrieked, and shouted, and probably swore in their own language. They were sprawled out all over the shuddering bridge, some crawling, others perfectly still. It seemed to be a regular shambles the wide-awake Serbs had made of that promising pontoon bridge. Instead of being "asleep at the switch," as one of the boys had hinted, it seemed that they had set a sly trap, and simply bided their time, waiting until the enemy had almost completed his work before setting out to demolish it.

Again the boys heard that larger gun somewhere close by give tongue. As they continued to stare as though spellbound they saw that this time the gunner had planned to smash the bridge half-way across. True had been his aim, for the missile cut a passage completely through the pontoons, leaving a gap some four feet or more wide there.

Josh gave vent to a cry; he could no longer suppress the emotion that seemed to be overpowering him. Unless he did something, or said something, he would begin to believe it must all be a horrible nightmare.

"Look, oh! look!" was what he exclaimed shrilly, forgetting all need of caution, for the guns were still grinding forth with that weird strain that, once heard, could never be forgotten; "they've smashed the bridge over there with that shell! This half of it is beginning to break up and float away with the current. It's all going to pieces, I tell you!"

They could see that Josh had not overestimated the terrible damage that had been wrought by that cleverly aimed shell. Deprived of its supports, the near end of the line of pontoons had already yielded to the drag of the current and was beginning to pass down-stream. As it went it also commenced to break into smaller sections. Here a boat sank, having been pierced by some of the numerous bits of flying metal. Again others broke away and floated off by themselves, often with dead or living freight.

The whole surface of the water seemed to be dotted with innumerable fragments of what only three minutes before had been a splendid specimen of engineering skill. The Serbs had waited until just the right time to strike their blow. They had made it felt, too, for the Austrian losses must have been terribly severe. More than that even, the injury to the morale of the dual kingdom's troops must have counted for a whole lot, while renewed confidence would be the portion of the defenders of the southern bank.

It was almost like a strange dream to some of the boys. Buster, who had gazed at the wonderful spectacle with distended eyes, might have been noticed to pinch himself violently on the leg, as though hardly able to believe that he was really awake and looking at such a picture of war's horrors.

The firing had mostly stopped by now, only that big gun sent another shell over, and succeeded in cutting another third of the pontoons loose, to be carried down-stream in a state approaching chaos.

Once again did darkness fall like a merciful curtain upon the scene. The boys were glad to have its horrors shut out from their sight. Never so long as they lived would they be likely to forget that smashing of the pontoon bridge.

CHAPTER XIX

THE AFTERMATH OF BATTLE

"Was it real, and did we see that bridge knocked into flinders?" asked Buster, when the terrific racket had in the main died out and it was possible for them to exchange comments or ask each others' advice.

"As genuine as anything that ever crossed our path," replied Josh. "Ugh! wasn't it fierce, though, to see those poor Austrians crawling like ants all over the old thing when it began to break up? Some of them were badly wounded, too. I tell you, we'll be seeing that sight many a time when we wake up from a bad dream."

"But what are we going to do now, fellows?" George wanted to know.

"The way is clear again," suggested Josh, helplessly.

"And will be right along to-night, unless those Austrian engineers try to shove out another lot of their pontoons, to be smashed into kindling wood," George said.

"There they begin firing again!" exclaimed Buster, in a fresh tremor; "oh! I wonder what's in the wind now."

"It's all from over the river on the Austrian side, you notice," Jack remarked, after the crash of a shell had been heard not a sixth of a mile below them and apparently close to the bluff that marked the river's edge.

"They're as mad as hops over the smart way the Serbs knocked their bridge down, seems like," suggested Buster.

"That's where your head's level, Buster!" exclaimed Josh; "if they can't have the game go their own way they won't play in the Serbs' back-yard. So now they're meaning to shell the river bank over here."

"What for?" asked the fat chum wonderingly. "They can't see a single one of the Serbs' batteries, or even a man for that matter."

"But they've located the different spots where that hot fire came from, and are hoping to get a few of the enemy guns with their big shells," continued Josh, who could always be depended on to do the explaining when he grasped a subject himself.

"Well, then, I do hope they won't drop a shell over this way and give us a bad scare," said Buster.

"That's a fact; that gun by which the bridge was cut to pieces did get in its work from near by here!" added George uneasily.

"I heard men talking and horses whinnying between the bursts of firing," said Jack; "so I reckon they cleared out just as soon as their work was done. That's the case, too, all along the line, the batteries and their supporting columns falling back to new positions so as to avoid the bombardment they know mighty well is going to come."

Sitting there in the boat, they watched the fitful flashes of fire on the ridge far back from the river. It was much more thrilling than any storm they had ever seen; and then would come the crash as each enormous shell exploded on the southern side of the hotly contested stream that served as the border between the hostile countries.

Once there was a frightful detonation not far away from where the boys huddled aboard the little motorboat. The Austrian gunners had commenced to send missiles toward the spot from which the Serb gun had barked. Doubtless a terrible hole had been knocked in the bluff, a cavity that looked like a crater resulting from the explosion.

Every one of them had felt the shock attending the bursting of the high explosive shell, though luckily none of the fragments chanced to scatter in their direction.

"Oh! that was an awful crack!" groaned Buster, as though his heart might have tried to jump into his throat and partly choke him. "I do hope they won't give us an encore. A hundred feet further this way and our name would have been Dennis."

"Huh!" grumbled George, "better say it would be Mud, because we'd have gone into the river with tons of the earth here."

"Listen! The Serbs are replying now!" said Jack.

"And that gun sounded exactly like the one that knocked the bridge to bits," added Josh.

"Let's hope, then, the fellows across on the hills there recognize its bark!" George exclaimed with considerable fervor, "and realize that it isn't around this region any longer. Then they won't bother wasting any more of their ammunition in bombarding this place."

Apparently this was just what happened, for that shell was not followed by others, much to the relief of the boys. Buster in his heart even forgave the Austrians all they had done to nearly frighten him to death because of their forbearance now.

"No use wasting your good stuff any more, Mr. Austrian General," he announced, "because the bully little Serbs have been too smart for you.

They shot their bolt and then changed partners, just like you might do in dancing the Lancers. So call it off and settle down again."

The firing still kept up, however.

"They've got oceans of ammunition up there," remarked George, "and have been just aching to expend some of it, which is why they keep on whanging away when they haven't any more chance to hit anything than you'd meet with in finding a needle in a haystack."

"But they won't try to keep it up all night long, I hope?" Buster observed.

"Not much danger of that," Jack told him, knowing the other was fretting.

"I wonder if the boy and his kid sister will manage to get into Belgrade, and also find their mother alive?" Josh went on to say, showing that even in the midst of all that horrible confusion he could let his thoughts stray to the pair whom they had so generously assisted in their great trouble.

"We'll hope so, anyway," George added, for he, too, had been greatly drawn to the winsome little lassie with the bright eyes, now able to see as well as any one.

"I can see lights moving across the river and low down," announced the keen-eyed Josh just then, and his words gave Buster a thrill.

"My stars! I wonder if those stubborn Austrians are meaning to tackle the job again and try a second bridge? They may have a new lot of pontoons, you know, and want to use them. Some people never can take a hint, it seems, and that one from the Serbs was as strong as anything could be. 'No trespass' was the sign they nailed to that bridge when they scattered it over the water."

"'Keep off the grass,' you'd better say, Buster," corrected Josh whimsically.

"I hardly think they're reckless enough to make another attempt at this place to-night," Jack told them. "When they get ready to try again it will be in a locality further removed from Belgrade. They can always hope to catch the Serbs off their guard, you know."

"But then what are those lights moving around over there for?" demanded Buster.

"You can see others further down the river in the bargain," Josh explained. "In my humble opinion they're looking up their wounded, and trying to pick up any who managed to swim ashore below."

"You notice that the Serbs are not interfering with them at all," Jack continued, "which goes to show they believe just as Josh here said, and that it's the Red Cross corps working along the river bank."

"I guess the Serbs feel satisfied with what they've done to-night," was George's comment. "Not only have they smashed the bridge of the Austrians, but must have killed and wounded hundreds of the enemy. All this with little loss to themselves. It's going to make them feel their oats, let me tell you."

"Still Austria is so powerful that sooner or later a force three times as big as the Serbian army can be thrown across the Danube to invade the country. When it does come to that, though," added Josh, "I give you my word for it, they'll fight like tigers."

"You notice that the firing is dying down again, don't you?" asked Jack.

Only an occasional shot still sounded. When it did come the deep grumbling echoes rumbled back and forth between the opposing heights until they died away in softer cadence in the distance.

"How will we go from here, Jack?" questioned George. "Will it be safe to start up the engine while we're so close by?"

"I was studying that very thing, George," replied the other, "and had about made up my mind that it would be much better for us to repeat what we did before."

"That means push out with the pole, and let the boat float on the current, eh, Jack?"

"After we get a mile or two further down the river we can think of using a little power and increasing our speed. But this is dangerous ground, you know," was what the skipper went on to say.

Buster knew that the time was coming, and very soon now, when they would again be on the move. He was glad of it, and yet at the same time viewed the approaching change of base with fresh anxiety. So many perils seemed to yawn in front of them, and all with ominous aspect.

He stared out upon the darkened river, though, of course, it was little he could see. Still, to Buster just then it was peopled with enemies of every type, men in boats moving around seeking trouble, and ready to strike hard at the first sign of opposition.

Buster found himself between the two horns of a dilemma; he wanted to get away from there, and at the same time hated to incur fresh perils. As generally happened with him, in the end he decided to put himself entirely in the hands of his three mates and let them settle the matter as they thought fit.

Which was possibly the best thing Buster could have done.

By the time another ten minutes had crept past Jack began to bestir himself.

"Is it time?" asked Buster dubiously.

"The firing seems to have stopped entirely," he was told, "and if that's the case, the sooner we're out of here the better."

Of course, there would be Serb sentries posted all along the river bank, unseen in the darkness, but ever vigilant to detect and report anything suspicious that might take place. On the other hand, some of the Austrians might have put out in boats stationed below on purpose, meaning to search for wounded men among the floating fragments of the pontoon bridge.

Once Jack put some of his strength into his work and they could feel the boat gliding away from the shoal water where they had been lying quietly for such a length of time.

Buster drew a long breath, and tried to pierce the gloom by which they were surrounded. If there was anything he hated it was that sense of impending evil, with not the slightest chance to ward it off. Still he got a grip on himself, and determined that if the others could stand it he must do the same.

CHAPTER XX

A RESCUE BY THE WAY

As soon as they were out a short distance from the shore the ever-present current took hold of the boat, and they found that they were beginning to move down the river.

Jack worked hard at his task. He knew it would be to their advantage to get as far away from the bank as possible before passing the places where the Serbs had lain in ambush. There would be less danger of their presence on the water being discovered in that case.

Josh hovered near by. Unable to resist the temptation, he finally took hold of the pole while Jack was pushing, and "leaned on it" in a way to render considerable assistance.

Everything seemed to be working in a satisfactory manner so far as making good progress went. If it kept up for a few minutes more Jack believed they would have achieved their end.

A single shot coming from further down the river on the northern bank gave him some little cause for uneasiness lest the fierce bombardment break out again. It proved to be a false alarm, since nothing followed, the Serbs never even taking the trouble to respond to the invitation. They had taken up new positions, and apparently were averse to letting the enemy "feel them out."

Now they must have reached the place where the swaying bridge made of heavy planks laid upon successive pontoon boats had a short while before been in the process of completion.

It gave the boys a queer sensation to remember this. Over the spot which they were now passing had swept that hurricane of missiles, mowing down the engineers engaged in bridge building as though they might be wheat falling before the reaper.

All was clear now, not a sign of the recent dreadful engagement being visible. Further down the river doubtless there would be met with fragments of the wrecked bridge. Jack knew that later on they would have to keep on the lookout for all such obstacles to a safe passage; but there would be little or no danger up to the time they started the engine and increased their pace.

About that time, when all of them felt exceedingly nervous over the possibility of being fired upon, possibly Buster may not have been the only one of the little party who called himself a fool for having accepted this risk.

It was too late now for vain regrets, however; they had made their beds and must lie in them.

"Well, we're past that awful place, anyway," whispered Buster presently; and no doubt, while the others did not echo his words, they felt just about as the stout chum did.

"Do you know," Josh was saying cautiously, "the way that bridge went to pieces made me think of a house of cards when you blow at it."

"Please don't talk any more just now," asked Jack; "we're still too close to the bank, and you might be heard."

"Correct!" said Josh, which in his vernacular was as much as asking Jack to excuse his break.

After they had floated along for some time, and Jack figured that they must by then have covered all of two miles, he decided it would be safe to start the engine. Of course, this could not be done without more or less popping and similar noise, try the best he was able; but Jack figured that the Serbs would not open fire for several good and sufficient reasons.

In the first place, they knew they had nothing to fear from one small launch, no matter if it were an enemy craft. Then again, as the Austrian Red Cross was undoubtedly searching for victims of that fusillade, there was a chance that this might be one of their units pursuing a mission of mercy.

Accordingly Jack started things up.

The engine responded readily to treatment, much to the satisfaction of Buster, who had been entertaining serious fears. The motor had proved tricky on one other occasion, he remembered, and on this account he wondered what they would ever do should it go back on them again.

They were now in the war zone, and it would hardly be possible to get repairs made and secure permission to continue down the Danube on their cruise.

Of course, Jack did not think to put on a full head of power; that would hardly have been wise while they were apt to come upon floating remnants of the bridge at any time.

"Josh, you can help me now if you want to," he presently told the other.

"Give your orders, then, Commodore."

"Crawl up forward, and keep as close a watch on the water as you can," Jack told him. "I mean directly in front of us, because it might get us in trouble if we ran smack into one of those pontoons out here in the middle of the river."

"I get your meaning, all right," responded Josh, starting to carry the plan out. "I'll call myself the lookout man, and signal you to back her in case I see any sign of trouble ahead."

"Give a sharp whistle, and I'll know what that means," the skipper told him.

So Josh crept past Jack and sprawled there in the extreme bow. He possessed good eyesight, and was likely to discover any floating object long before they were in danger of striking the same.

Buster, too, strained his eyes in order to try and supplement the good work; but George contented himself with lolling there in a comfortable position. What was the use, he doubtless figured, of everybody getting excited? If later on Josh wanted some one to "spell" him George would be quite willing to assume the responsibility; but he did not mean to wear out his eyes when not on duty. And no doubt George was quite right.

Things were going on so well that every one felt much encouraged. Buster was even trying to figure on what sort of speed they were making, and where they would arrive if able to keep on at this pace all through that night.

"Jack said it was about a hundred miles down to the Iron Gate," he told himself, "where the river makes a turn and starts to divide Serbia from Rumania. Wonder if we could make half of that between now and morning, and what would we do through the day? I must ask Jack first chance I get if he thinks it would be safe for us to keep on down the river by daylight, with soldiers guarding every mile of the banks and ordering us to come ashore and explain who we are."

Just then Buster gave a sudden start, for Josh had whistled sharply. Jack instantly cut off the power and then started to reverse the engine so that their headway might be reduced to next to nothing.

"Steady, Jack; we're going to come alongside a pontoon that seems to be partly filled with water!" said Josh in a stage whisper.

He leaned still further over the bow, as though bent upon reaching out to fend off from the object that was floating like a derelict upon the bosom of the great river.

"I've got it all right, fellows," Josh continued saying; "and would you believe it, there's a wounded man in the same! Guess he'd have gone down in less'n ten minutes only for our coming along."

"What's that you say, Josh?" asked Buster eagerly, "a wounded man! How do you know but what he's dead?"

"Because he's sitting up here," came the prompt reply.

Jack knew what that meant. They could not leave a poor fellow badly injured to go down with the leaking pontoon.

"We've got to get him aboard here, that's flat!" said George, as though voicing what was passing through the mind of each of his chums just then.

Jack left the wheel and, passing along the side of the boat, leaned over. Yes, there was a man in the sinking pontoon. He did not appear to know whether they would turn out to be friends or foes; but his situation was desperate, and upon seeing several heads appear in view he commenced saying something in a weak voice.

"That's Magyar, of course," remarked George; "but the trouble is none of us can translate a word of the same. However, that doesn't make any difference. Shall we help him over the side, Jack?"

"Three of us can do the business, easy enough," responded the other.

When the Austrian engineer realized that they meant him to leave his wretched float and clamber into the motorboat, he lost no time in starting to obey; though his actions quickly told them he must be very weak, either through loss of blood or from the shock of his wound.

Once he was deposited in the cabin, Jack sent Josh again to the lookout, and himself started the engine. The man had sunk upon the cushioned seat as though quite content to take things as he found them. He heard these unknown parties speaking in what he must have known was English, and was no doubt much astonished. Just the main thing with him was being rescued from the fate that had been threatening him with a watery grave.

"Jack, he's pretty badly hurt, I reckon," suggested George soon afterward.

"Well, something ought to be done for him, that's certain," the skipper started to say. "Do you think you could manage it, George? I don't want to give up the wheel, and Josh is really needed forward there."

George did not hesitate long. He guessed that it might be anything but a pleasant task, but then George had learned long ago not to shrink because things were not always delightful.

"I'm willing to do the best I can, Jack," he said quickly.

"I knew you would, George, and there's not one of us can dress a wound better than you, once you set your mind to the job. Get Buster to help you, George."

"Sure I will," spoke up the stout chum, "though I'm not clever at handling sick people, and always shiver at sight of blood. But you'll need some kind of light to work by, won't you, George?"

"Wait," said Jack. "You remember I've got that little vest pocket electric torch. I've been saving it because I'm afraid the battery will soon run out. But this is just the time to make use of it."

He thereupon handed Buster the article in question, a small nickeled affair not over three inches in length. When the button was pressed there came a shaft of light that was fairly strong.

"Just the ticket, Jack," announced George, who was removing his coat with a business-like air that quite tickled Buster, who thought George already seemed to take on a professional look.

They could now see that the man taken from the sinking pontoon was a young Austrian soldier. He had no marks on his uniform to prove him anything save a private, but that made no difference to the boys. They had seen how those engineering corps men had taken their lives in their hands in order to bridge the Danube so that the artillery might be transported across to the other bank, and had also watched them going down by scores when that furious fire burst out from the hidden Serbian trenches. On this account they must honor him as a brave man.

He knew what George was about to do. Perhaps, after all, taking off his coat was the sign that made his intentions clear to one who could not understand English very well.

Buster shut his teeth hard when the light focussed on the man showed that one of his arms was bloody. Still he did not quail, for Buster could do a thing once he put his mind to it.

George set to work. The Austrian soldier understood that he was to help as well as he could, and between them they managed to get the water-soaked coat off. Then the sleeve of his shirt was carefully rolled up, disclosing the wound.

It was enough to make one with a stouter heart than Buster shudder, for the cut was severe, and had bled a great deal. From his pack George took some linen bandages, without which his mother would not have let him leave home. He had other appliances in the bargain, among which was surgeon's adhesive plaster, with which to keep the ends of bandages in place.

First of all George proceeded to wash the wound, Buster getting him some water from the river in a tin basin they carried. After that he applied the soothing salve that was intended to purify and take away some of the pain that would be sure to follow on the morrow.

Jack glanced in every little while, and saw that George was getting on splendidly, having tied a tourniquet above the wound in order to stop the bleeding. He was now engaged in winding a bandage tightly around the arm in a most professional way.

The man appeared to be very grateful. He said something once in a while, but as none of them could understand a word of Magyar they had to guess at its meaning. Actions speak louder than mere words, however, so they knew that the patient appreciated their efforts in his behalf, and that he was trying to tell them as much.

Finally, to the great relief of Buster, the job was done, and the man had his coat on again, though that left sleeve hung empty at his side.

"And I want to say, George," remarked Buster, as he shut off the light and handed the little pocket torch back to the owner, "that you did the job up as neat as wax. If ever I have the misfortune to get jabbed by a bullet I want to engage you as the chief surgeon right now. I'd feel myself in good hands, all right."

Of course, this pleased George very much. It was not so very often that he did anything to call for such fulsome praise; but he knew Buster meant every word he uttered, because Buster was candid and sincere.

"I'm beginning to wonder what will strike us next," George went on to say. "We are sure neutral in this world war, because one day we hold out a helping hand to a couple of young Serbs in trouble, and right afterwards pick a wounded Austrian out of a sinking pontoon and look after his hurts."

"Well, that's the way it goes," asserted Buster, with a philosophical air. "You never can tell what will happen, and especially when there's a silly old war on. We may run across others who are clinging to fragments of that bridge until we gather up a boatload."

"Then there'd be nothing else for us to do but run over to the Austrian side of the river and land the whole bunch," George told him.

Josh meanwhile had kept a good lookout. Several times he sighted other pontoons and floating planks, but as they did not happen to be in the direct way of the motorboat he had not given the warning whistle to cause Jack to stop.

He had watched in every case to ascertain whether there happened to be occupants to these boats, but discovered none. If men had floated away on them when the Serbian gun smashed the bridge, they must either have made their way to the shore and been taken off by search parties or else gone down into the depths.

By degrees, however, these reminders of the dreadful tragedy became fewer and fewer until Josh failed to discover any more of them. From this he decided that, owing to the increased momentum attained for the motorboat by the use of its engine, they had by this time distanced all drifting snags. Still he clung to his post until another ten minutes had elapsed, when he came back to where Jack sat.

"We've got beyond all the floaters, Jack," he remarked, "and anyway my eyes begin to feel the strain. So I thought I'd just drop in and find out what your plan of campaign might be."

"Do you mean for to-night?" asked the pilot at the wheel.

"Sure thing, Jack. We're moving right now at a healthy pace, but how long do you mean to keep the same up, I'd like to know?"

Jack took a look aloft. He found that the same conditions prevailed there, with the heavens covered with clouds so that the moon was entirely shrouded from view.

"If things continued like that up there," he assured Josh, "I'd feel like keeping on the move the whole night long. We'll have to hide somewhere in the daytime so as to keep from getting into trouble; and perhaps to-morrow night we can cover the balance of the distance separating us from the Iron Gate."

"But how will you be able to stand it?" demanded Josh, indignantly.

"Oh, I can make up for lost sleep to-morrow, you know; there'll be really nothing else to do the whole day long but sleep. And if I find myself getting too dopey for any use, why, I can call on George or you to take hold. It's all right, Josh, and please don't waste any pity on me. I'm only too glad to be able to cover half that hundred miles before dawn comes on."

Josh knew better than to dispute Jack when his mind was made up. Besides, that arrangement just suited his own ideas.

George had been listening to this talk, also Buster.

"I don't call it fair for you to take all the burden on your shoulders, Jack," expostulated the former; "especially when the rest of us are willing to do our part."

"Oh, so far as that goes, George," he was told, "you're all under orders, you know; but if I get tired I promise to call on you for help."

CHAPTER XXI

A HALF-WAY STOP

Time passed, and the motorboat continued to swing along with the current hour after hour. Jack did not attempt to make great speed. There was no necessity, and such a move would be doubly dangerous, on account of possible snags, and also discovery from the shore.

In spite of their resolve to stay awake, Buster and Josh and George seemed to be enjoying a pretty healthy nap. The wounded stranger also lay very quiet. Jack hoped he was not in too great pain.

It was a long, dreary spell of duty for the boy at the wheel. When finally George did manage to awaken and, sitting up, asked Jack if he meant to let him take a turn, he was considerably astonished to hear the other say:

"I hardly think it would be worth while for me to lie down just now, George, because, you see, the night is nearly gone, and any minute we may have to be turning in to the shore to look for a cove where we can stay during the day."

Both of them watched closely for an opening. If the Danube was anything like the rivers they were accustomed to in their home land an occasional little bayou was likely to occur, an indentation in the shore line where possibly some creek emptied its waters into the greater stream.

If only they could find some such a friendly harbor it was Jack's idea to push the motorboat in and remain secreted during the entire day. He had an idea that the region they were now passing through was rather wild and not settled very thickly, which fact was apt to please them considerably.

Josh happened to wake up about this time and wanted to know what was going on. When he was told that morning was not far distant he could hardly believe it until Jack asked him to notice where the moon had gotten far over in the west, for it was possible to locate the heavenly luminary behind the clouds.

"All right, then," he remarked, after George had informed him what they were bent on doing, "there's your little crook in the shore just ahead of us."

"You've certainly got the eyes of a cat, Josh," George told him; "because it is what we're looking for, as sure as anything."

Jack was already making use of the setting-pole to urge the motorboat toward the shore. As the current proved very mild close in, he did not have much difficulty in doing this.

They managed to enter the cove, for such it proved to be. As far as they could see in the wretched light it was surrounded by thickets and lush grass.

"Just the sort of place we wanted to run across," remarked George; "and the celebrated Stormways luck still holds good, it seems."

They soon had the boat fast to the bank. It was then that Buster sat up and commenced yawning at a terrific rate.

"Here, what's going on out there?" he asked cautiously. "Have we got fast on a sandbar? Do you want any help pushing off?"

When he crawled out from the cabin he stared around him as though he could not understand it.

"What! gone ashore so soon, after all, Jack?" he remarked reproachfully.

"So soon?" echoed Josh. "Why, do you know it's nearly morning, boy? All of us just slept like logs and let Jack do the work. I feel like kicking myself, that's what."

"Let me do it for you then, Josh?" asked Buster. "It'll help wake me up good and plenty, you know."

"Thank you, but I'm capable of doing my own kicking most of the time. But Jack, now that we've landed, you get in under the shelter and make yourself comfortable right away. We'll wake you up later on when we've got breakfast ready."

"That's right, sure we will," added Buster vehemently, though he looked disappointed because Josh placed such little confidence in him.

"Of course, I needn't ask you fellows to look out for our passenger," remarked Jack. "He seemed to sleep a part of the time, though I heard him groaning once or twice, poor chap. Be sure to cook enough breakfast for an extra boarder when you're about it, Buster."

With that Jack consented to lie down. He was asleep before five minutes went by, being fairly well exhausted. When they aroused him two hours later it was long since full day. The clouds, too, were breaking overhead, promising fair weather, a fact that pleased them all very much.

Breakfast was ready, and the odors gave promise of an appetizing meal. Jack discovered that George had looked again at the arm of the injured Austrian, though not removing the bandage, as everything seemed to be getting along nicely. The man appeared to be rather cheerful. He could say a few words of English, and managed to understand that they were American boys to whom he found himself indebted perhaps for his very life, certainly for the many comforts he was now enjoying.

After they had partaken of breakfast and satisfied their keen appetites, the boys sat around and talked in low tones. Josh, while Buster was getting the meal, had gone ashore and roamed around a little. He reported that so far as he could see the place was quite lonely.

"I discovered the house of a Serb peasant," he explained. "There are only an old man and woman home, as their boys have been called to the colors to fight. They seem to be well disposed and can speak some English. I told them who we were and what we were doing on the river. I also took pains to speak of the Serbian boy and girl we helped get through the lower part of Austria and landed near Belgrade. They say we are all of fifty miles away from the capital now."

"I figured we must have covered something like that last night," said Jack confidently; "and another similar turn would take us to where we would have no need of feeling worried. I was thinking that perhaps we might influence this couple to take our patient off our hands and keep him until he can get across the river again. A couple of dollars would be something worth while to them, you know."

"We'll try it, anyhow," ventured Josh. "Another thing, fellows; I bargained with them to have a chicken killed and dressed for our dinner. If we do have to hold over here, there's no reason why we should go on half rations."

As the morning advanced they began to hear the far distant sound of heavy firing again. This, of course, held their attention more or less, for they had come to take a personal interest in the warfare between the would-be invaders and the gallant Serbs, who stood ready to defend their shore from attack.

Not feeling just like lying down again, Jack accompanied Josh over to the humble cabin home of the old peasants. They managed to talk with them, partly through the sign language, by means of which so much can be exchanged between two people neither of whom can speak the other's tongue.

Jack found that the old people were not at all bitter toward Austrians as citizens, their resentment being only for those in high places, who they believed desired the ultimate annexation of all Serbia in order to link the Teutonic races with Turkey and the East, where Germany believed the star of destiny was drawing her, with the rich booty of India in her eye.

They readily agreed to care for the wounded engineer corps man until such time as he could get across the river again to his own country. Later in the day the boys brought the Austrian to the cabin and saw him installed there. George had made a stout sling for his wounded arm, and on the whole the man felt that these young Americans had treated him splendidly.

So they had again "cleared the decks," as Josh put it. First the Serb brother and sister, and next the injured bridge-builder who had been swept away in that hurricane of fire when the concealed Serbs smashed the pontoon structure.

All they meant to wait for now was the coming of night. They could eat an early dinner, for Buster had that fowl all cut up and ready for the frying pan. With the coming of darkness after the gloaming they meant to start forth, take the middle of the river, and make as fast time as the conditions warranted.

All of them were glad to see the sun sinking toward the western hills. During the afternoon there had been no vigorous firing in the distance, though once in a while they would catch a faint boom. It was just as though the contestants wanted each other to know they were still watchfully waiting.

No doubt the Austrians would have other plans to try and carry out. Because the first pontoon bridge had been wrecked was no reason they would not exert themselves to effect a crossing. History tells us that in the end they did succeed in transporting an army to Serbia, and for some time pressed the men of the valiant old King Peter back along the valley of the Morava; but once among the hills and wilder country so suited to their style of fighting, the Serbs, with the old king at their head, struck heavy blows that brought consternation upon their enemies. In the end the Austrians were compelled to begin a retreat that savored almost of a rout, so that for months afterwards not a single invader remained on Serbian territory.

Buster had supper ready on time, and it was a royal feast. He had gone ashore to where the obliging Josh had built a splendid cooking fire, and here Buster had an opportunity to spread himself.

By the time supper had been finished and everything cleaned up it was beginning to actually grow dark. Jack was keeping track of the time, and also of the attendant conditions.

"We ought to leave here in ten minutes or so," he said. "The moon, being some past the full, isn't to be looked for until about nine o'clock or later to-night. That's going to give us an hour and more of darkness to make our first run. After that we'll have to take Hobson's choice."

"The moon is going to shine bright enough," observed Josh; "but as the river is getting pretty wide down here, and we can keep to the middle, it's small chance of our being seen from ashore. Besides, there are few soldiers around this part of the country, the old man said."

When the ten minutes mentioned by Jack had passed the word was given, and once more the motorboat began descending the dark waters of the Danube.

CHAPTER XXII

CONSTANTINOPLE AT LAST—CONCLUSION

That was another night of constant watchfulness. Some one would have to be on duty every minute of the time they were in motion, to handle the wheel and keep the motorboat as near the middle of the big river as possible.

The moon shone brightly at times, and again hid her face behind friendly clouds. But they were at a good distance from either shore, and objects even in the full of the moon are never distinct. A peculiar little haze, too, hung over the water, making things seem very romantic, and helping Jack and his chums wonderfully.

Jack changed his plan of campaign on this second night. He decided to sit out the first hour or two and then resign in favor of George, who in turn might be followed by Josh, though the last mentioned was not as much of a skipper as the occasion called for.

The worst of the danger Jack believed was past. It lay in that quarter where the Austrians had expected to force a passage of the Danube by means of a pontoon bridge, over which, their heavy guns could be taken. There would undoubtedly be more or less peril all along the border, for not a mile but would have its watchers, eager to report any activity on the other side. Still Jack hoped to pass almost unnoticed, if fortune were kind.

This programme then was carried out, George being put in charge of the wheel about ten o'clock, with orders to call the skipper if anything suspicious came to pass. This might consist of any one of a dozen different things; and George felt that his honor was at stake when he took command of the expedition, so it could easily be understood he was wide awake.

Just two hours afterwards Jack sat up. He had been sound asleep all that time, and, considerably to the surprise of the wheelsman, awoke at the very time he said he would.

They sat and chatted in low tones for a long time. Nothing happened to alarm them, and the boat kept constantly descending the widening Danube. At times the shores came closer together as the country assumed a wilder aspect, with mountains bordering the romantic looking stream. Occasionally they could see dim lights on one side or the other, which would indicate that they were passing some village or town.

It was well toward morning when Jack awoke the others. Long before this George, who had been yawning tremendously, decided that it was unnecessary for him to try and sit Jack out. If the skipper were bent on keeping the wheel constantly, what was the need of any one else losing their full quota of sleep? And so George had lain down again, though protesting to the last that he didn't think it quite fair.

When Jack awoke them it was with a word of caution.

"We've got to the Iron Gate, fellows," was what he told them, "and I thought you would be sorry if you didn't have a chance to see for yourselves. Besides, there's more or less danger for us in the next half hour, so I concluded you ought to be on deck. No talking now, please, but watchful waiting."

They sat there and counted the minutes as the boat passed between what seemed like high bluffs. George could easily understand now why the place was called the Iron Gate. Bulgaria's nearest border lay only thirty miles away, but the intervening country was so rocky and wild that an army would have a frightful time trying to force its way across the strip, especially when such valiant fighters as the Serbians manned the heights.

Nothing happened, however, and later on Jack calmly announced that they had made the turn in safety upon which so much depended.

Instead of Austria, they now had Rumania on their left, and as that country was at peace with Serbia, there was little occasion for believing the shores would be manned by troops or batteries.

Jack consented to go and lie down as the faint streaks of coming dawn began to appear in the east. He had been under a heavy strain, although his manner was so cheerful that one would never suspect it; and he certainly needed a good long rest.

They did not wake him up for breakfast, acting on his orders. This frugal meal Buster prepared while they were going at full speed down the constantly widening river.

So the morning passed. At noon Jack made his appearance and announced that he felt like a new man again. George, who had been skipper for the time being, refused to resign his post of honor until dinner time had come and gone. Tired of being on board, they found a good retired place and went ashore to prepare this meal, as well as "loaf" for an hour or two in the heat of the day.

Long before night came on they had left turbulent Serbia far behind and found themselves running between Bulgaria and Rumania.

Two days later found them at the bustling Bulgarian river city of Rustchuk, and here they rested for fully twenty-four hours, laying in a few more stores and trying to learn something of the great events that were happening in other parts of Europe.

It was here they heard that the Belgians had stood like a stone wall in front of the Kaiser's legions, ten times their strength, delaying the advance for days at terrible cost to themselves, so that possibly the German hosts might find their long arranged plan for taking Paris nipped in the bud.

The boys also learned of other great events, beginning with the news that Great Britain was now at war with the Teuton allies, together with word of a Russian advance into East Prussia.

All these things interested them intensely. Being right there on the ground, and having lately actually been in the whirlpool of the war, they could understand and appreciate the tremendous nature of the world-wide struggle much better than any of their friends, who were separated from the theatre of conflict by thousands of miles and could read of battles without a thrill.

The voyage was resumed after a time spent in the Bulgarian city, and presently they found themselves headed almost due north, such are the vagaries of the wonderful blue Danube in its long journey from the northern border of Switzerland all the way to the Black Sea.

They were now in Rumania proper, and four days later arrived at the important city of Galatz. Here they expected to say good-by to the motorboat that had served them so well on their long and eventful trip. Arrangements had been made for turning the same over to a certain dealer, who was instructed to repay Jack the amount of security the boys had been compelled to put up against possible loss of the chartered craft.

It took them the better part of a week to reach their port, for the steamer was what might be called a coasting trader, stopping at numerous towns on the Bulgarian and Rumanian shores for half a day at a time.

Nevertheless the boys enjoyed it immensely, though one night a little storm did come along and give Buster quite a scare. Fortunately, it died down before any damage had been done, though showing them how savage a sea could arise in short order in this inland body of water.

Finally they reached the entrance to the Bosphorus, and found themselves passing along a narrow stretch of water that filled them with delight. It was bordered with green groves, white buildings of rich Turks, occasional fortresses, and in places arose the domes of magnificent mosques, with their accompanying minarets, where at certain hours the meuzzen's loud call to prayer could be heard, summoning the faithful Mahometans to worship.

Then came Constantinople, where they meant to spend several days before starting for London via Italy.

Here they had the time of their lives, prying into all sorts of strange places, and seeing just how the red-fezzed Turks lived. All of them enjoyed it to the full, and no doubt laid up a treasure of recollections that would haunt them the balance of their lives.

Buster was wild to see the inside of a mosque the first thing, and managed to accomplish it with his mates, though all of them had to remove their shoes and put on ridiculous red slippers without heels, for the sacred interior of the temple would be profaned if shoes were worn.

Josh had gotten it in his head that he would love to see what a harem looked like, and came near getting into serious difficulty in pursuing this fad; but he never reached his goal, and had to give it up.

All the same, the boys looked upon a myriad of strange sights, such as they had read about in books like the Arabian Nights, but never really expected to see with their own eyes.

Jack noticed that there were a great many Germans in Constantinople, and he expressed the opinion that sooner or later he believed Turkey would align herself with the Teuton powers against her old-time friends and backers, Great Britain and France. His prediction was later on fulfilled, as events proved, and eventually Turkey took the mad plunge into war at the behest of her master, Germany, to submit her last slender grip on European territory to the test of the sword.

Here in the wonderful city on the Golden Horn we will say good-by to the four Motorboat Boys. They fully expected to start for Italy in two days, and were now only filling in the time waiting for a certain steamship to arrive that would convey them through the Sea of Marmora, along the historical Dardanelles into the Ægean Sea, and finally to Naples, where they could at their pleasure sail for London and home.

No doubt our adventurous young friends, whose fortunes we have followed with so much pleasure in this and previous volumes, are bound to meet with further stirring experiences, which in due time we shall hope to lay before the reader. Until that time arrives we shall have to drop the curtain and write the words.